"I'm really getting married."

Logan's emerald gaze focused on her. "Oh, no." Alison's voice was faint. "It was bad enough when I thought you only wanted us to masquerade as an engaged couple. But to actually *marry*... No."

Logan's voice was brisk and businesslike. "I'm afraid the marriage will have to be legal. "It's just that it won't be *real*. Or, at least, not long-lasting. If you'll do this one little thing for me, Alison—"

She shook her head in disbelief. "Getting married does not exactly fall under the heading of a simple favor!"

"—I'll make sure you end up with a baby."

Dear Reader

I've always enjoyed writing books which are connected—sequels, prequels and spin-offs. They usually come about because a secondary character in one book is so interesting that he or she demands a story of their own! But until now I've never tackled an interconnected set of books, so the **Finding Mr Right** trilogy has been both a challenge and a joy. And I'd like to thank the partners of the all-woman public relations firm in Kansas City, who provided the inspiration for my setting.

I'd also like to thank you, my wonderful readers, for following me through the fifteen years since my first book was published. I think you'll enjoy meeting Kit, Susannah and Alison as much as I enjoyed writing about them. I warn you, though—I cried when I had to give up these three special new friends...

THE HUSBAND PROJECT

BY
LEIGH MICHAELS

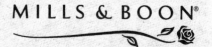

First published in Great Britain 1998
Harlequin Mills & Boon Limited,
Eton House, 18-24 Paradise Road, Richmond, Surrey, TW9 1SR

© Leigh Michaels 1998

ISBN 0 263 81307 X

Set in Times Roman 10 on 11.5pt.
02-9812-54224 C1

Printed and bound in Norway
by AIT Trondheim AS, Trondheim

CHAPTER ONE

EVERYWHERE she looked, there were babies.

In the supermarket, they cooed and grabbed at bright-colored packages. In the park she passed each day on her walk to work, they toddled through tall grass and dug in the sandboxes. In the office of one of her clients, a set of twins napped cherubically on a blanket behind the enormous walnut desk...

Despite what she was seeing, however, Alison Novak knew that the Windy City hadn't actually had an abrupt population explosion. Human beings had a tendency to see what they looked for, and she was no exception. As soon as a person became acquainted with a new word, she was apt to see it everywhere from billboards to telephone books. Likewise, as soon as a woman realized how urgently she wanted a baby...

It was the first time she'd admitted that her longing for a child had gone beyond desire all the way to desperation, and the realization twisted Alison's heart into a pretzel. As if in answer, the pain which had for weeks been coming and going in her abdomen flared sharply. This one was worse than usual; it shot clear through to her back and brought tiny beads of perspiration to her upper lip.

Abruptly, she changed her mind about going back to the office and turned into Flanagan's instead. The small neighborhood bar was quiet and cool, and she could sit there for a few minutes till the pain calmed, as experience told her it would.

In any case, it was just half an hour till her partners would be joining her; the three owners of Tryad Public

Relations met at Flanagan's every Friday evening for brat-wurst and a wrap-up of the week's work. With any luck, by the time Kit and Susannah arrived, this attack would have passed and Alison would be back to normal.

She sank into a booth not far from the front door and asked the waitress for a glass of seltzer water with a slice of lemon. As Alison waited for the drink to arrive, she leaned her head against the tall back of the booth and closed her eyes, focusing her attention inward. Though the pain was a little worse than it had been before, it was following the same basic pattern—starting off like the worst stitch in her side she'd ever felt, and gradually diminishing as she sat still. This time it seemed to be concentrated on the left.

She was so intent on analyzing the discomfort that she didn't see the waitress bring her drink, and she didn't re-alize her partners had arrived till she heard Susannah's voice coming toward the booth. "It's perfectly awful, that's what it is.... Are you taking a nap, Ali?"

Alison opened her eyes and sat up a bit too suddenly; the dim little bar seemed to revolve for a moment, and Susannah's face, full of concern, swam before her eyes. "I'm fine. What's so awful, Sue?"

Susannah flung herself into the seat beside Alison. "The single most valuable piece of art the Dearborn Museum owns was vandalized this afternoon."

"The Evans Jackson painting?" Alison was startled. "How could anybody vandalize it?"

Across the table, Kit choked and started to laugh. "You sound almost like me, Ali. I wanted to know how anyone could tell it had been damaged. It was nothing but smears of red paint on a white canvas in the first place, so—"

"That was *not* what Ali asked," Susannah said firmly, and turned to Alison. "Somebody sneaked a can of spray paint into the museum and made a few additions."

"Maybe it'll actually increase the value," Kit murmured.

"You have no appreciation of modern art."

"Neither do you, so don't be a hypocrite, Sue."

Susannah looked stern for only a few more seconds before she burst into giggles. "That's true. And actually, I have to admit—only to you guys, of course—that it did look better. At least there's some variety now. However, when anything that's insured for half a million gets damaged, it's.... Why aren't we in our usual spot, Ali?"

"Fresh air." Alison waved a hand toward the propped-open door. "Fall's coming fast, so we'd better enjoy this while we can." *That wasn't bad for thinking quickly,* she told herself. She wasn't about to admit that ten minutes ago she hadn't felt like walking another step.

"It is warm in here," Kit agreed. "Though you look a bit pale, Ali. You didn't walk all the way back from downtown, did you?"

Alison shrugged. "It's rush hour. If I'd tried to get a cab I wouldn't be here yet."

Susannah slid to the far end of the bench seat, turning to stare at Alison with her eyes narrowed. "If it was the walk, she'd be flushed instead of pale, Kit."

Kit's eyebrows rose. "You're right. Then—"

Susannah picked up the glass of wine the waitress had set before her. "And it's not just today, either. Ali's been pale for a couple of weeks. I've always thought she looks sort of like an old-fashioned china doll, all shiny black hair and porcelain complexion—but there are limits."

"And one of my limits is when you talk about me as if I'm not here," Alison reminded. "Anyway, I'm fine. I'm just a little tired from a long week."

She didn't think she'd been terribly convincing, for Kit's eyebrows remained elevated and Susannah's blue-green eyes watchful. But to her relief neither of them pushed the question.

Kit drew circles on the table with the base of her soft

drink glass and said, "Sue and I have some great ideas for getting the singles club up and running, Ali."

Alison sighed. "Look, guys. I'm sorry, but you know very well I've been no more than lukewarm on the idea of the singles club since Sue first came up with it."

"You're the one who suggested getting a restaurant to sponsor it," Susannah pointed out. "And that's the key to—"

"One suggestion hardly makes me a fan. And I can't do a good job on a project I think is ludicrous."

"Oh, really?" Kit murmured. "What kind of public relations person are you, anyway? We're *always* doing something ludicrous. If you think I want to brag about creating a bunch of dancing ducks to promote the new water park—"

"But you believe in the water park," Alison reminded.

"Doesn't matter. Besides, you can't expect either Susannah or me to do it. You're the only one of us who can, Ali."

Alison sighed. "Because I'm the only one of us who's still single."

"Exactly," Kit murmured.

"That is completely illogical, you know. It's like saying I can't make a good video welcoming newcomers to Chicago unless I'm a newcomer, and that's just—" There was no warning this time, and the pain which racked her was by far the worst she'd ever experienced. Alison clutched at her abdomen. She'd have doubled up, but there wasn't room in the narrow booth.

Susannah's gaze met Kit's. "An ambulance, do you think?"

"No!" Alison struggled to sit upright. Almost automatically she said, "It'll pass."

"Sure of that, are you?" Kit sounded skeptical.

"It always has before."

"Oh, *that's* reassuring! How long have you been feeling this way, Ali?"

"Weeks," Susannah said darkly. "Remember, Kit? Clear back when you started having morning sickness, Alison was—"

If she hadn't been feeling so wretched, Alison would have burst into laughter at the sudden suspicion in Susannah's eyes. "I'm not pregnant," she managed. "It's just…cramps or something. A little worse than usual, but—"

"I'm relieved to hear it, Ali," Kit said crisply. "Excuse me for missing the occasion, but just when *did* you get your medical degree?" She didn't wait for an answer. "We're going to check this out right now. If you'll go get your car, Susannah…"

Susannah didn't move. "Are you sure I shouldn't call the paramedics?"

"I'm not sure of anything," Kit said. "But we can't ride with her in the ambulance, so we'll need the car anyway." She dug her cell phone from the depths of her handbag.

Susannah nodded and hurried toward the door.

"Oh, for heaven's…" Another wave of pain swamped Alison's voice.

Kit flipped madly through her address book. "I knew I should have put this number on auto-dial."

"I don't want an ambulance, Kit."

"I'm calling a friend."

Alison, taken aback, could only stare at her. *A friend?*

"A friend who also happens to be my obstetrician."

"I told you, I'm not—"

"—Pregnant, I know. Well, obviously there's something wrong, and the way you're clutching your tummy makes it a good bet that you'll end up consulting somebody in that field. Besides, Logan's the only doctor I can think of who's likely to still be in his office after six on a Friday night…"

She turned her attention to the telephone. "Hello, is Dr. Kavanaugh in? I see. Will you page him and ask him to call Kit Webster? It's an emergency."

The worst of the wave had passed, and Alison could get her breath again. "I'm too busy for this. I've got a video to finish..." She was startled by the high, tight pitch of her voice and the panic which clutched her throat.

Kit put the phone down. "Exactly. And if you'd stop to think about it, Ali, you'd realize that I'm only doing this because I'm darned if I want to get stuck finishing your video." The words were tart, but her smile was warm and reassuring.

Alison's panic eased a little, but the lump in her throat suddenly felt as big as the Sears Tower. "Yeah, right," she said. "Kitty, I don't deserve you and Sue."

"Can we get that in writing?" Susannah said breathlessly. "I'm parked on the sidewalk, Kit, so it might be a good idea if we don't hang around here much longer."

Kit's phone rang and she turned away to answer it.

"I can walk," Alison said.

Susannah looked doubtful, but when Alison pushed herself to her feet, Susannah quickly offered her arm. Their progress was slow, hampered not only by Alison's discomfort but by Flanagan's other patrons, crowding around to offer advice.

They were almost to the car when Kit caught up. "Now that's luck," she said briskly. "Logan's at the nearest hospital, just finishing a delivery—so he'll meet us in the emergency room."

Alison sank into the back seat. There was no comfortable position; what she wanted to do was draw her knees up to her chest and howl. In a feeble effort to distract herself, she said, "Was his delivery a boy or a girl?"

"I didn't stop to chat," Kit said dryly. "For all I know it could have been a Federal Express package."

In the emergency room, Susannah went off to deal with the paperwork, and Kit waited outside the small treatment room while two staff members swarmed over Alison to do a preliminary examination. It was only after they had left and quiet descended on the room that she really realized where she was, and what was likely to happen.

Time to face the truth, she told herself. *You were an idiot in the first place to try to pretend nothing was wrong. Now you can't pretend anymore. And if your nightmares turn out to be fact after all—*

Alison's heart seemed to be skipping every other beat as fear pumped adrenaline through her veins. She tried to keep her eyes so tightly closed that the tears couldn't seep out, but it was impossible.

Kit took her hand. "Another one?" she said gently. "Squeeze as hard as you need to, Ali."

Alison shook her head. "No. I'm just…so stupid. Thinking that if I pretended it didn't hurt, it would stop."

Kit said slowly, "And if you didn't see a doctor then nothing could really be wrong? That's a first-class case of denial, Ali, and I could just—" She took a deep breath. "No, this isn't the time for a scolding."

Susannah appeared in the doorway. "Why not? Sounds to me like she deserves one." She brushed a lock of Alison's perspiration-dampened dark hair back from her temple. "It'll be all right now."

It might never be all right again, Alison thought.

Susannah's grin was mischievous. "I can promise that because I just caught a glimpse of your doctor, and let me tell you, Ali, you're one lucky girl."

A rustle from the doorway made both Susannah and Kit move away from the side of the examining table. Restlessly, Alison turned her head.

Lying flat on her back, looking almost directly into the bright overhead lights, was hardly the best way to get a good view. Even so, Alison had no trouble figuring out what Susannah had been talking about. Her visual perception might be skewed and a good part of her attention focused on her pain; nevertheless, she realized with her first glance that her new doctor was one of the best-looking men she'd ever seen.

He was tall and broad-shouldered; the washed-out green scrub suit which would have been baggy on another man fitted him as easily if it had been tailored. His hair was an unruly dark brown thatch, just a little longer than it ought to have been. His face was angular, with a strong jaw and a mouth which hinted that he liked to smile.

She looked up into his eyes. They were green—a deep, true green that Alison had never seen before—surrounded with indecently long and curly lashes.

He was surveying her every bit as closely, but for different reasons; Alison could almost see the calculator in his brain checking off symptoms even before he offered a hand, large and capable and tanned. "Ms. Novak? I'm Logan Kavanaugh," he said. "Tell me when you started to feel this pain."

He listened with his head tilted just a little to one side, jotting notes from time to time on the clipboard he carried, those brilliant green eyes seeming never to leave her even when Kit interrupted now and then with more details. Then he laid the board on a nearby cabinet and said, "And it hurts…right here, is that right?"

Alison was sure that under normal circumstances the pressure of his hand on her abdomen would have been no more than a firm touch. As it was, however, she felt as if a cannonball had hit her squarely where she hurt worst. She screamed, and her body instinctively folded up into a fetal position.

If she'd been lying on her side, there would have been no awkward consequences from simply pulling her knees up tight to her chest and bending her head protectively over her vulnerable midsection. Instead, she was on her back, with Logan Kavanaugh bending over her—and as she reared up off the table, her forehead collided with his jaw. Her vertebrae rattled with the impact.

He staggered back from the table, one hand pressed to his face. "I see I found the right spot." His voice was level, but when he took his hand away from the corner of his mouth, his fingers were red. "Excuse me a moment."

As he left the room, Alison lay back on the table. The pain in her abdomen was almost relentless, and now her head ached, too. Even breathing hurt.

"Now that was a full-speed retreat," Susannah said admiringly. "You're a wonder, Ali. I'd never have come up with such a novel way to get rid of a man." She moved closer to the table and patted Alison's hand.

Despite the pain, Alison couldn't keep herself from laughing—though it sounded more like a sob.

In less than a minute Logan Kavanaugh was back, holding an ice cube wrapped in a piece of gauze against his lip. He stopped a full pace from the examining table. "What have you eaten today?"

Alison closed her eyes. "A light and early lunch. So if you think, *Doctor,* that this is nothing more than indigestion—"

"No, and I'm sure it's not hunger pains, either. I think it's the hottest appendix I've seen in years. I've already called a surgeon, but we may as well get the basics out of the way while we wait. Are you allergic to any medications?"

Alison shook her head wearily.

Kit said, "But is it safe to wait, Logan? Couldn't you—"

"What? You want me to voluntarily spend an hour in the same room with her and a scalpel? She's dangerous enough with only her head as a weapon." His voice was full of lazy humor, but Alison bristled anyway. "It won't take long for the surgeon to get here," he went on, more seriously. "By the time we've done the workup—"

"It's not appendicitis," Alison said.

A silence as clear and hard as crystal fell over the room. From the hall came the sound of footsteps and lowered voices, but inside the examining room the only sound was the nagging hum of the clock above the door.

"I beg your pardon, *Doctor*," Logan Kavanaugh said. His imitation of the ironic note in Alison's voice was precise. "And just what is *your* diagnosis?"

Susannah said hastily, "She's not herself. Really, Dr. Kavanaugh. She's practically out of her mind with pain."

"Ali." Kit sounded tired. "You haven't been reading medical books, have you?"

"What an incredibly idiotic question," Susannah said. "The research queen of metropolitan Chicago? Of course she has—she probably keeps *Gray's Anatomy* on her bedside table right next to her *Dun and Bradstreet*."

The door opened, and a white-coated woman with short red hair and a sprinkling of freckles appeared, her hand already outstretched for the clipboard Logan Kavanaugh held. "Thanks a bunch, Kavanaugh," she said absently as her gaze dropped to the chart. "You know I have a date tonight. At least, I used to have."

Logan Kavanaugh shrugged. "You shouldn't be hanging around with that guy anyway, Sara."

She ignored him and smiled at Alison. "I'm Sara Williams, and I'm a staff surgeon here. If I can just take a look…"

Logan's ice cube had melted and the piece of gauze had been thrown away, but his index finger went as if by instinct to the swollen bump on his lip. "You might want to be careful doing that," he said under his breath.

"Go away, Logan," Dr. Williams said briskly.

He didn't, exactly; Alison was dimly aware that he stopped in the doorway to talk to Kit. But she wasn't paying attention to the low-voiced conversation; a moment later one of the nurses returned to give her a shot, and within a couple of minutes her tongue wouldn't work right and nothing seemed to matter anymore.

Alison remembered only snatches of the hours that followed. The pain wasn't gone, but it was different—no longer knife-sharp, but a sort of dull burn that haunted her whenever she broke through to consciousness. She tried to hang on to wakefulness, because the physical ache was better than the anesthesia-induced dreams; she didn't remember them exactly, only the feelings they left behind, and that was bad enough. But despite her efforts, she kept sinking back into the twilight like a swimmer caught in an undertow.

Finally, though, she opened her eyes to see dim lights, the standard equipment of a regular hospital room, and Susannah bending over her, talking soothing nonsense.

"What are you doing here?" Alison managed to say. "It has to be the middle of the night."

"Just about." Susannah sounded cheerful. "I am the night shift, standing guard."

Alison closed her eyes, but this time she didn't sink like a rock into unconsciousness. "Why?"

"Because Kit and I were afraid you'd try your hand at nursing—and if you're as bad at that as you are at diagnosis, you'd be gangrenous by morning."

"Then..." Alison swallowed hard. "It *was* appendicitis?"

"Of course it was. Why were you so sure it wasn't?"

"The pain was in the wrong place. And there were a whole lot of other reasons, too." The knot inside her stomach—the leaden lump which had settled there the day she'd first looked up her symptoms in her layman's medical guide—slowly loosened, and once more she sank into the depths. But this time her sleep was more natural, and she wasn't haunted by the dreams.

By morning the whole thing felt like a nightmare, except for the lingering effects of anesthesia and the fact that she could barely shuffle across the room, even if she held on to an aide with one hand and the stand which held her intravenous drip with the other. But Alison gritted her teeth and refused to quit.

At midafternoon, she paused to take a rest in the marginally-comfortable chair in her hospital room, her back propped with pillows so she could get up by herself when she was ready for her next walk down the hall. From her window she could see little but a dusty courtyard surrounded by plain brick walls, but Alison wasn't interested in the view. She was retracing her state of mind over the last few weeks, remembering how each occurrence of pain had increased her fear and each release had allowed her to pretend it couldn't happen again.

For an intelligent woman, she told herself, *you certainly have been acting like a fool.*

She didn't even look around when she heard the knock on her half-open door, just called, "Come in."

A moment later Logan Kavanaugh pulled a straight chair up beside her. Today the green scrubs had given way to easy-fitting charcoal trousers and a white shirt with faint gray pinstripes. "I just stopped in to see how you're doing."

"I'd rather be at the football game."

He grinned, and his dark green eyes sparkled. "Wouldn't we all?"

Alison looked at him a little more closely. Under the humor in his face, she could see the marks of tiredness;

there were lines around his mouth and faint shadows under his eyes. And, she noted with a tinge of guilt, there was not only still a tiny bump on his lip, but she could see the half-inch-long red line of the cut. "I suppose you've been delivering a baby?"

"Now and then," he said. "I think the count stands at seventeen since my last day off—but it's possible I've forgotten a couple. It's been a very long week."

"You're on duty all the time?"

"In theory, no. But—for instance—a few months from now, when Kit goes into labor, can you imagine what she'd say if she called to tell me and I said, 'Good luck, I'm sure you'll like the guy who's on call, and I'll stop in tomorrow to check on you'?"

"Point taken."

He leaned forward, elbows on knees and hands tented together. "I also came in to apologize for my unprofessional behavior yesterday."

Alison frowned. "I don't quite—"

"For one thing, making that crack about not wanting to be alone in a room with you and a scalpel. Though I was only your doctor for about three minutes, and I'd technically turned you over to Sara by then, I shouldn't have said that."

"You had reason to be provoked. I'm really sorry about your lip." Alison took a deep breath. "Look, thanks for seeing me yesterday. You're obviously very busy, and I know I wasn't exactly an ideal patient."

"You mean because you wanted to argue about the diagnosis? Just out of curiosity—what did you think it was?"

She looked out the window. "I'd eliminated everything except ovarian torsion."

"Oh, that's interesting. It's not at all common for an ovary to twist, you know, and it's just about as dangerous as an acute appendix."

"I know," she said, and drew a deep breath so she could go on.

A hint of laughter crept into his voice. "That must be an extremely detailed medical guide you've got—or has the popular press made torsion the disease of the week?"

Alison was furious. "I am not a hypochondriac, Dr. Kavanaugh," she said tightly. "I didn't cast around for an interesting disease, I simply looked up my symptoms, and that's what I found. I'm an intelligent and informed woman—"

"—Who doesn't know the difference between an appendix and an ovary, but thinks she's an expert anyway."

"What was it you were saying just now about unprofessional behavior?" Her voice dripped sweetness.

He ignored the interruption. "Do you have any idea how close you came to—" He shook his head, rubbed his hand across the back of his neck, and stood up. "Never mind. I'll let Sara jump on you about the risk you took by not seeing a doctor till it was almost too late. She's getting paid to yell at you about taking proper care of yourself. I'm not. Goodbye."

Forgetting her incision, Alison tried to leap up from her chair, and fell back, eyes wide, too startled even to swear. She sagged back against the pillows and tried deep breathing to ward off the stab of pain.

Logan had left the door standing wide open, so Kit didn't knock. She burst in, dumped an overnight bag beside the bed, and leaned over Alison to give her a gentle hug. "Now this is more like it. You've even got some color back, I see. I met Logan in the hallway, but he seemed to be in a hurry. You didn't slug him again, did you?"

"I didn't slug him last time, either," Alison pointed out. "It was an accident." She eyed the overnight case—the last time she'd noticed, it had been on the top shelf of her bedroom closet—and raised an eyebrow at Kit.

"Your purse was still in Susannah's car, so I stole your keys," Kit said blithely. "I figured the cats needed feeding—"

Alison winced. "I can't believe I forgot about my cats."

"I not only fed them, I played with them—which is why I'm so late. And I picked up some clothes for when you're ready to go home." Kit perched on the edge of the bed. "I brought your medical guide, too. I thought you'd probably want to read it again, in light of the new developments. If you like, I could try to catch Logan so he can show you where you went wrong."

Alison rolled her eyes. "No, thank you. That man is incredibly egotistical."

A voice from the doorway corrected her. "That man is incredibly good." Sara Williams strolled across the room, chart in hand. "Feeling better? The nurses tell me you're doing quite well, so there's no reason you can't go home. There are a few restrictions, of course—the discharge nurse will give you a list. Do you live alone?"

Alison started to nod, but Kit intervened. "I'm taking her home with me for a few days."

The doctor nodded approval, and hardly a moment later she was gone. Kit shook her head. "And I've always thought Susannah was a whirlwind," she muttered.

"I can manage on my own, Kit. You don't have to baby-sit."

Kit had stooped to pick up the overnight bag. Very deliberately, she set it on the end of the bed and turned to Alison. "Sometimes, Alison, you don't seem to need anybody at all."

The somber note in Kit's voice brought tears to Alison's eyes. She tried to blink them away, furious at herself. Surely she wasn't going to turn into a wet sponge, dripping all over the place at the least provocation! Quietly, she said, "Thanks, Kitty. I don't want to go home alone."

As they drove across Chicago to Kit's lakeside high-rise, Alison wasn't listening to her friend's chatter. She was still hearing the unusual soberness in Kit's voice as she said, *Sometimes you don't seem to need anybody.*

But I do, Alison thought. *I need somebody to love.*

From the guest room of Kit's condo, Alison stared down at the enormous expanse of Lake Michigan. The water was clear and blue under the morning sun; a light wind whipped up gentle frothy waves and bulged the bright sails of the armada of boats—at least a hundred of them. Alison could count so many not only because the condo was so high and the air so clear she could see almost all the way across the lake, but because the effort of taking a shower had worn her out so thoroughly that all she could do was drop into the armchair by the window and rest.

Eventually, however, she pushed herself up from the chair, put on a set of soft knit exercise clothes, and walked down the hall to the kitchen.

Kit looked up from the chopping block where she was dicing green onions and ham. "Good morning, Ali. How about an omelette?"

"You don't need to pamper me." Alison dropped into a chair beside the breakfast bar. "Surely you've got enough to do with your brunch to prepare."

"You're certain you don't mind? I can still cancel it, you know."

"No, you can't. When you invite ten people for brunch, you can't change your mind two hours beforehand."

"They'd understand." But Kit sounded a little less than convinced.

"Well, I wouldn't. You've had this planned for weeks. Cancel and I'll really feel like I'm imposing on you."

Kit shrugged. "You already know better, so there's no

point arguing about it. Shall I set a place for you? You're looking much better this morning.''

"And make your numbers odd? Now that *would* be a disaster," Alison teased. "I'll spend a couple of hours lying in one of those canvas chairs on the terrace, hiding behind a ficus tree and reading a book. So party on—you won't disturb me a bit, and your guests won't even know I'm here."

The terrace was beautiful; it stretched the length of the Websters's spacious condo and looked out over the lake. Alison chose a chair on the corner just outside the guest room, as far as possible from the elegant living room. If Kit's brunch guests spilled out onto the terrace, she'd have plenty of warning, and she'd just slip quietly back into her bedroom.

She tried to read, but the light novel she'd found on the guest room shelves didn't have the power to draw her in. Instead she found herself gazing at the waves, forming and breaking in a hypnotic rhythm, rolling toward the horizon as they always had and as they would, for eternity.

Eternity. She'd come a little closer to it yesterday than she wanted to think about, and of course there wasn't any need to dwell on that, now. The danger was over, and she'd been very, very lucky.

However, the reason she'd put off seeing a doctor—the reason she'd hidden behind denial instead of taking care of herself—was just as real now as it had been a few weeks ago when she'd picked up her medical guide, looked up her symptoms, and realized the threat which hung over her head.

The threat that she would no longer be able to have a child.

Alison would never forget the sick horror of that instant. She'd always known, of course, that she wanted a child—at least one, maybe several—but she hadn't realized till then exactly how desperate that longing had become.

When she stopped to think about it, however, the timing made perfect sense. Her two best friends were focused on family right now; with Kit celebrating her first pregnancy and Susannah newly married and starting to think about children, the subject resounded throughout Tryad at the drop of a paper clip.

With all that going on, it was no wonder Alison's biological clock had started to tick. The oldest of the trio by a couple of years, she was getting uncomfortably close to thirty. If she was going to have a child at all, the time was soon. It was no wonder she'd been so frightened when her medical guide suggested that she'd already put it off too long.

But fortunately her fears hadn't been real. Once her recovery from the surgery was complete, she'd be in her normal excellent health. There was no reason she couldn't have a child.

Of course, there was one minor problem. She was unmarried, and there were no prospects in sight. Which wasn't to say there weren't plenty of men in her life—but that was a different matter.

She got up from her chair and went to lean on the waist-high wrought-iron terrace rail, thirty-five stories above the lake. *Kit will have a hard time child-proofing this place,* she thought idly. It would be far easier to make her own row house safe…

Absorbed in her daydreams, she didn't hear footsteps coming slowly across the terrace.

A deep, soft voice was the first warning that she wasn't alone. "Not thinking of climbing over that fence, are you?"

Startled, Alison twisted to face him, forgetting her incision.

Logan Kavanaugh crossed the intervening distance in a couple of steps and slipped an arm around her.

He'd actually put on a jacket and tie for Kit's brunch party, Alison noted, even as she said irritably, "You don't have to restrain me. I'm not suicidal."

"That's good. Sara told me she took particular care to leave you a scar that'll look cute with a bikini, and I'd hate to see her work wasted."

Alison rolled her eyes. "I'll bet."

He hadn't let go of her, she realized. His arm was still around her shoulders. She could feel the rough tweed of his sleeve even through the lightweight knit of her exercise suit. And was it a sudden warm lake breeze which stirred the hair at her temple, or his breath? He seemed to have forgotten how close he was standing.

Well, that problem was easy to fix. She'd give him her best glare and say something cutting...

She looked up at him, and in the split second before she opened her mouth she saw the answer to her problems.

"Dr. Kavanaugh," she said abruptly. "Will you help me have a baby?"

CHAPTER TWO

ALISON was absolutely certain of one thing; no amount of sarcasm could have made him let go of her any more quickly than that simple statement did.

Logan's arm dropped as if he'd suddenly realized her shoulders were coated with acid, and he backed away till he was leaning against the terrace rail, a safe distance from her. A casual observer would no doubt think his professional control was undisturbed, for his face was calm. Alison knew better; she could see the incredulity in those brilliant green eyes.

"For heaven's sake," she said testily. "You're a doctor who specializes in women. You must know how—" For the first time, she realized that there was an entirely different interpretation to her question than the one she had meant.

He obviously saw the double meaning hit her, for a sparkle of humor appeared in his eyes. "If you're asking whether I know where babies come from, I am familiar with the basics."

"I'm sure that's quite a comfort to your patients." Alison's voice was chilly. "Let's get this straight, however. Don't flatter yourself that I had you in mind as a potential father."

"And *that*," he murmured, "is quite a comfort to me. Do I understand that you want to use a medical procedure usually reserved for infertile couples in order to have a child?"

Alison relaxed just a little. "That's it, yes."

"Well, excuse me if this is a stupid question—but why not just go about it in the old-fashioned way?"

"I don't see any need to explain. Will you help me or not?"

He looked thoughtful. "Without an idea of what's going on inside your head? I'd sooner bodysurf across Lake Michigan on a stormy day."

"And if I explain?"

"Depends on the explanation. To be perfectly honest, I'd still put the odds at about seven to three against, but I'm willing to listen." He folded his arms across his chest and settled his hip against the terrace rail as if he was prepared to stay there all day.

Alison drew a long breath, hesitated, wet her lips. It shouldn't be so difficult to say the words, she told herself. Her reasons made perfect sense; any intelligent person could surely understand why she'd come to this conclusion. But her tongue felt numb and three times its normal size.

Partly, she realized, her paralysis was because of the way he was studying her. The last time he'd looked her over, in the emergency room, he'd been watching for symptoms. Now he wasn't—unless of course he suspected she was a mental case—and though his gaze was no more personal, it was an entirely different kind of survey.

And she was entirely different, too. She wasn't twisted with pain, flat on her back, her hair mussed and sweaty and her face stark white. She wondered what he thought of the difference.

He shifted slightly against the wrought iron. "If you're going to tell me that there isn't even one man in your life, forget it. I don't buy it." Another man might have give the line a suggestive twist, or turned it into a compliment. Logan made it sound like the stock report.

Annoyed, Alison said, "Of course there are men in my

life. In fact, that's part of the problem—there are too many men.''

His eyebrows soared. ''Oh, this ought to be good,'' he muttered. ''No, let me guess. They'd all be hurt if you chose one of the others, so to keep things in balance you're looking for an anonymous donor. Of course, this makes perfect sense.''

Alison glared at him. ''I have an incredible number of male friends,'' she began. ''The key word being *friends*. I'd like them all to still be friends when this is over. If I had even a short-term affair with one of them, the whole situation would change.''

''Well, now that you mention it—''

''Once there's a more intimate relationship, it's impossible to return to real, ordinary friendship.''

''And there's not a single one of your friends you'd sacrifice for the cause?'' Logan murmured.

''There's also the problem that whichever man I chose would know he was the father of my child, and that could create all sorts of difficulties.''

Logan snapped his fingers. ''I have it. If you expand this short-term affair to include *all* of them, everybody would still be on equal terms with you, and none of them would know who—''

Alison raised her voice. ''This is hardly the sort of professional discussion I was looking for, Dr. Kavanaugh.''

''Not even *you* would know. It's the perfect—'' Logan broke off. ''Of course, I suppose they *could* all line up for DNA tests… Sorry. You're right, of course. I'll try to stay focused. Do go on.''

''The father of a child has certain rights.''

''To say nothing of responsibilities,'' Logan murmured.

''That doesn't concern me. Financially, I can support a child easily. I could even take a baby to work with me. And I have no doubt that I'll be a good parent.''

"Singular. Have you considered that maybe the kid would like to have a father, too?"

"Wouldn't they all? The fact is, some kids are better off with only one parent. In a good many cases it isn't having a single parent that's the problem, it's being torn apart by the conflict between mother and father."

Logan didn't seem to disagree; at least, he stayed silent.

"And I'd be better at the job than most. If you're worried about who will teach my little boy to pitch a baseball—I will. And I can do anything else that comes along, too."

He began to applaud. "Brava, brava!"

"I just want a child," Alison said mulishly. "I don't want to give some man the right to interfere in my life—and my child's—for the next eighteen years. I don't want to mess around with every-other-weekend visitations and arguments about when the kid needs a haircut. Is that so unreasonable?"

"Obviously you're going to tell me why it isn't," he murmured.

"I'd gladly agree never to ask for financial support in return for a promise not to seek parental rights."

"Now you're talking. I suspect a lot of men would think that kind of a deal was pretty inviting—they could have all the fun and none of the responsibility."

"But that's just it. I know my promise is good, but how could I know *he* meant what he said? And even if he felt that way now, how could I be certain it would continue?"

"Make him sign something," Logan suggested.

"Do you honestly think that would do any good? If he came back in a year or two or five and wanted to mess up my child, what's going to stop him from suing me? All you have to do is read the front pages to know it's a lot harder for the courts to terminate a father's rights than it used to be. Even adoption isn't always final these days."

"Alison, this is a charming argument, but—"

She raised an eyebrow. "Excuse me, but I haven't suggested you use my first name. Or do your patients call you Logan?"

"Quite a number of them do. In any case, it's a moot point, since you're not my patient and you're not going to be."

Disappointment trickled through her. "You won't help me?"

"Even after hearing all your so-called reasons, I still don't see why you need medical intervention to carry out the most natural process on the face of the globe. Besides, I've decided just now that as a patient you're more than I want to handle. I'll give you my card, and you can talk to my nurse for the names of some other doctors who might be more inclined to cooperate."

He moved away from the terrace rail, reached for his wallet, and extracted a business card. But he didn't hand it to her; to Alison's utter astonishment he picked up her hand and raised it to his lips. "I must thank you, however, for taking me into your confidence. It's been—"

If he said *entertaining,* Alison thought, she'd kick him in the kneecap.

"Truly memorable," Logan murmured. He put the business card in her palm, folded her fingers over it, smiled down at her, and was gone.

The walk from her row house to work had taken longer than she'd expected, so Alison was later than usual when she climbed the front steps of the brownstone which housed the offices of Tryad Public Relations. And though she wouldn't have admitted it even under torture, she was far shakier than she'd expected to be. It was taking longer to snap back after her surgery than she'd thought it would.

From the porch next door, the twin to Tryad's, Alison heard a soft scuttling sound as Mrs. Holcomb retreated into her house. Though Tryad's offices had been next door, sharing a common wall, for three years now, Mrs. Holcomb still obviously considered Alison a stranger. And though the woman was no longer the textbook example of a recluse—in fact, she'd loosened up quite remarkably since the days when no one ever saw her outside at all—she still scampered for cover if surprised. But at least she'd speak to Kit and Susannah from time to time.

The idea that the old lady might actually be a bit afraid of her piqued Alison. ''I'm just as nice as Kitty and Sue,'' she muttered. ''You'd think she'd give me a chance, at least.'' She smiled at her own self-pity—why should she expect Mrs. Holcomb to be the one who made the first move?—and pulled open Tryad's front door.

It felt like a year since she'd been there, though it was scarcely more than a week. Alison stopped just inside the door to get her breath and bask in the quiet atmosphere she loved so well. Sunlight spilled through the stained-glass panel above the front door and lavishly spread a rainbow of colors across the beige carpet on the stairs and the golden oak floor of the hall. Upstairs, from the front office, she heard Kit's laugh. The aroma of fresh coffee wafted up from the ground-floor kitchen and mixed with the scent of photocopies still warm from the machine near the receptionist's desk.

As Alison came into the front office which had once been the brownstone's living room, the secretary jumped up, almost knocking over a vase of flowers. ''You're back!''

Alison fielded the vase and sniffed a half-open red rose. ''Very nice, Rita,'' she said. ''I hope the flowers are a romantic gesture, though, because if someone's sending bribes and trying to hire you away from us we'll have to do something drastic.''

Rita colored gently; her pink cheeks made her hair look even more silvery than usual. ''My son sent them for my birthday,'' she said. "I thought you were going to be gone another week.''

Alison shrugged. "I was very bored, and every time I tried to follow doctor's orders and rest, one or the other of the cats decided to jump up on my lap. Given the choice of sitting at a desk or having a Persian napping atop my incision, I decided I might as well come back to work.''

"Well, you look as if you're about to drop,'' Rita said critically.

"Will it make you happier if I sit down to read my messages?'' Alison took a thin sheaf of pink notes from the basket marked with her name. "There aren't many, for a whole week. And here I thought I was indispensable to the firm.''

"Those are just the personal ones, people who called here when they couldn't get you at home.''

Alison wasn't really listening. Most of the messages were short, just friends and clients offering a few words of encouragement and the wish that she'd be back in top form soon. But her friend Jake had called with a doctor-patient joke which Rita had patiently transcribed, right down to a punch line which made Alison groan.

And Rob Morrow had phoned to ask her to the opera. When he'd heard why she was out of the office, he'd left a tongue-in-cheek message that he'd heard some fancy excuses in his day but having surgery to avoid sitting through *Rigoletto* was the best one yet.

She smiled and put the sheaf of messages down. Just reading them had left her feeling warm and comforted. Her friends were special, indeed.

And there's not a single one of them you'd sacrifice for the cause? Logan had asked.

He'd sounded just short of sarcastic, but Alison was even more convinced that she'd been right not to turn to her male friends. She was genuinely fond of each of them, or they would no longer be in her life—and she wasn't willing to take any risks with those relationships.

Few males, she had found, were able to comprehend the simple concept that men and women could be friends without sexual feelings getting in the way. She didn't for a minute suppose that Logan Kavanaugh understood that, or he wouldn't have asked such an idiotic question.

But even among men who accepted the general principle, it was difficult to find one who could wholeheartedly translate that philosophy into his personal life. That was why she hadn't seriously considered talking to any of her men friends about her desire for a child. She suspected that, despite their good intentions, most of them would conclude that her request implied a whole lot more than a simple favor. And a good many of the rest would feel just a bit threatened since they hadn't been asked...

Alison realized belatedly that Rita was talking, her soft voice rhythmic and soothing. "Kit and Susannah have been splitting your business calls. Kit's taken everything to do with the video, Susannah's handling the singles group and..."

A low, warm voice from the hallway said, "Did I hear my name?" A moment later Kit was standing over Alison's chair, arms folded and one foot tapping ominously on the hardwood floor.

"What are you doing here? You aren't supposed to be driving yet."

"Who said I drove?"

"Then please tell me you took a cab. Because if you walked all the way over here—"

"Dr. Williams told me to get gentle exercise."

"I think she meant to start with a little less than half-mile hikes. Why didn't you call and ask for a ride?"

"Because you'd have told me to stay home." Alison

smiled at the look of defeat in Kit's eyes. "Anyway, I'm here now, so I might as well do some work."

She was extra careful on the stairs which led down to her office on the ground floor, since going down steps was still one of the more difficult things physically, and the last thing she wanted to do was take a pratfall with Kit standing by to say *I told you so.*

Susannah and Kit had offices on the upper floor, in what had once been bedrooms. But when they'd first toured the building, in the days when it was still a home, Alison had taken one look at the ground-floor study, with its thick walls and high windows and built-in bookshelves, and fallen in love.

She had never regretted her choice. Since it was half underground, the room was always warm and quiet, and being as far as possible from the confusion of the top floor production room was worth the effort of climbing all the way up now and then.

The surface of her black lacquer desk was exactly as she'd left it, bare except for her red leather blotter and a whimsical Chinese vase that doubled as a pen holder. Her projects were laid away neatly in the file drawer below, and she pulled out the most pressing of them. The promotional video she'd been working on for months, intended to draw industry to Chicago, was in the hands of the tape editors, but there was plenty to be done in the next couple of weeks while they finished the final cut.

And then there was the singles club. The outgrowth of a casual brainstorm of Susannah's months ago, the project had landed on Alison's desk only because Susannah hadn't found a sponsor until the week before her wedding. And how would it look to her new husband, she'd asked Alison earnestly, if she started spending a couple of evenings a month in a singles group?

So Alison had inherited the club—a project she still

thought was Susannah's craziest idea yet. But one of Chicago's finest restaurants had agreed to host and sponsor the club, and now there was no backing out; Tryad's reputation was on the line, and Chicago Singles would succeed, or else.

She opened the folder, and within minutes she was buried in her work. Even if her heart wasn't entirely in the project, Alison had to admit that the more deeply she became involved in the singles club, the more possibilities there were.

She didn't realize how long she'd been working till she stood up to get a notepad from the storage closet out in the hallway and had to grab the corner of her desk to keep from falling. She was light-headed, and there was a nagging ache in her lower back and a sharper one near the half-healed incision.

"So much for the idea that you don't need rest breaks any more," she told herself dryly as she evicted Tryad's calico cat from her comfortable nest at one end of the white wicker love seat. The cat glared and stalked off, tail high, and Alison lay down, wriggling around until she found a comfortable position.

The love seat was hardly conducive to naps—but then she didn't intend to sleep, only to rest for a few minutes. Kit had installed a chaise longue in her office, and Susannah had selected an overstuffed couch, but Alison had deliberately chosen the wicker love seat and matching chair because—while they were cozy and inviting with their feminine, frilly cushions—they were not so comfortable that visitors sat around just to chat.

Her brain kept on ticking, rattling off promotional possibilities for the Chicago Singles. She loved her work, so much that it didn't feel like a job at all most of the time. And she was comfortable with her life. Of course she wanted a child, and she'd continue to explore her options—but she must have been nuts to have gone off the deep end, that day on Kit's terrace. She must have still been in shock from her surgery—and from her fear of never having a baby—to have reacted so idiotically.

She hoped Susannah never heard about the incident. She was the one who specialized in crackpot ideas and who seldom thought them through to the obvious consequences. She'd have a good laugh about Alison—practical, logical Alison—asking a doctor to help her have a child…and asking on the spur of the moment, without even a thought for the outcome.

Her eyelids drooped, and her mind began to spin.

She didn't know what sort of a party it was at first. She couldn't hear anything, and everything seemed to be in black and white. Like an old home movie, that was it.

Slowly the picture cleared, like a projector coming into focus. Now she could see people, party hats perched on their heads, their mouths moving but making no sound. They seemed to be watching her; she glanced down and realized she was carrying a cake, balancing it carefully in both hands. A birthday cake from the looks of things, since there was a fat candle glowing in the center…

A single candle. She looked up eagerly, her eyes searching for the child the birthday cake must belong to. But the crowd of party-goers was dense. Suddenly, however, the group shifted, and people stepped aside to make room for her. At the end of the aisle they'd formed was a high chair, and in it sat a small child, romper-clad and wide-eyed, with a tuft of dark hair sticking straight up. Alison smiled and stepped forward, tripped over her own feet and went sprawling. The candle snuffed out an instant before Alison's face smashed the thick white icing…

She jerked awake and lay back against the cushions, breathing hard. "Talk about Freudian," she muttered finally, and pushed herself into a sitting position.

Yes, she'd been acting bizarre that day on Kit's terrace. It had been little short of insane to blurt out her wishes that way, and particularly to Logan Kavanaugh. When the only experience the man had of her was a sick, argumentative woman who'd left him with a sore and bleeding lip—well, it was no wonder he hadn't been eager to cooperate. She must have been deranged not to see that before she'd so thoroughly embarrassed herself.

But the fact she'd been crazy to bring it up to him didn't mean it was a crazy idea. Granted, she'd have been better off to think it all the way through first and do a little more research before choosing a doctor. But the longing was real; she still wanted a child. And the facts hadn't changed; all her arguments made just as much sense now as they had in the first burst of enthusiasm.

She'd been tempted to rip up his card, but common sense had made her hesitate. Why start from scratch if she could get a referral? And she wouldn't have to talk to Logan himself; he'd said himself that his office nurse could help…

She'd just dialed the last digit when Susannah's blond head appeared around the edge of Alison's half-closed office door. "Rita said you were asking about— Oh, sorry. Want me to come back later?"

Susannah's timing, Alison thought testily, couldn't possibly have been worse. She started to put the phone down.

Before she could break the connection, however, the line clicked and a low-pitched Southern drawl said, "Obstetrics and Gynecology Associates."

What a tongue twister. Somebody ought to have had better sense. Hastily Alison put the phone back to her ear. "I'm sorry. Wrong number." She hung up without waiting for a response. "I'm finished, Sue. Have a seat."

Susannah flopped down in the big wicker chair. "I kept a list of the calls I took for you and what I did about them— or mostly, what I didn't do." She handed a sheet of yellow paper to Alison. "The majority said their business could wait till you were back in shape."

Alison ran her eyes down the list. No big problems jumped out at her. "Thanks, Sue."

Susannah swung around and draped her legs over the chair's arm. "My pleasure. I also wondered.... You know the painting that was vandalized at the Dearborn Museum?"

Alison frowned. She remembered only vaguely—but her foggy recall made sense; Susannah had mentioned it at Flanagan's when Alison's pain was at its worst. "What about it?"

"The artist is coming to town to inspect the damage, and of course as the museum's official public relations person I'll have to be there. I wondered, if you don't have another obligation, if you'd go with me."

"Why? I've never been part of the Dearborn campaigns."

"Moral support," Susannah said firmly.

"Nobody can possibly think it's your fault, can they?"

"Of course they can. I'm the one who suggested that instead of a guest book they hang a plain white canvas and let visitors write their comments with markers. So when the board starts looking for a scapegoat, and remembers that I encouraged the patrons to write on things—"

"That's ridiculous."

"Since when did that prevent clients from yelling? A week from Saturday, five in the afternoon. Can you go?"

"I think so." Alison reached for her calendar. "That night's the first Chicago Singles meeting, so I'd have to go directly from the museum to Coq Au Vin. But maybe I can talk to the museum director about hosting an event for the stupid singles club."

"Better quit calling it that," Susannah advised, "or you'll slip one of these days. I can see it now, on some morning interview show on television... Are you going to have gift certificates for membership?''

''Hadn't thought of it.''

''If you do, I might get one for our painter friend.''

''He'd think it was a personal apology for the additions to his canvas.''

''You're probably right.'' Susannah yawned. ''Kit tells me you and Logan Kavanaugh not only connected—pardon the pun—at the hospital but you spent a whole hour tête-à-tête on her terrace.''

''Did she?'' Alison buried her face in a folderful of blank paper and did her best to sound entirely uninterested.

''So what's going on there?''

''Absolutely nothing.''

''Come on, Ali. Don't tell me you're just going to add him to your string of male pals.''

''Not on your life.''

Susannah sat up with the grace of a ballerina, grinning broadly. ''Aha! Now we're getting somewhere. If you don't want to be friends with the man, it must mean you're seriously attracted to him.''

Alison put the folder down with a snap and looked levelly at Susannah. ''You know, Sue, my life was a whole lot less complicated before both you and Kit went nuts and fell in love.''

''Mine, too, but it was much less fun. So when are you going to see him again?''

''I'm not.''

''Really?'' Susannah rose slowly. ''Then why were you calling him at the office just now? I heard the receptionist answer. That's a terrible name for a medical practice, don't you think?''

Alison choked.

''And why, instead of admitting it, did you hang up on the poor woman when I came in? What, I wonder, didn't you want me to overhear?'' Then Susannah smiled like an angel and walked out without waiting for an answer.

The thinness of the stack of messages waiting for her on Rita's desk had been a mirage; the fact was that every client Alison possessed—including some she hadn't heard from in a year—called in the next week. Caught between too much work and the lingering effects of her surgery, Alison even considered installing an air mattress in her office. The main reason she didn't was that she couldn't find time to call the store and arrange a delivery.

She yawned as she climbed the steps to the main floor, carrying the final draft of yet another letter to be personalized and sent out to a mailing list of hundreds. She'd leave it on Rita's desk to be taken care of in the morning, and then she was going home.

Used to the bright lights in her office, Alison was startled by the dimness on the main floor. She'd known it was late, of course—she'd drawn the curtains over her office windows hours ago, and the stillness of the entire brownstone had told her everyone but she and the calico cat had departed. Still, she'd expected the last bit of twilight to still be trickling through the windows at the head of the stairs. Instead, there was only the yellow light which spilled from the entrance porch through the beveled glass panels around the front door.

She flipped the hall lights on and crossed toward Rita's office. A shadow moved on the steps outside, and Alison's heart jolted. Tryad's hours were clearly posted on the door; why would anybody be lurking outside now? A public relations office wasn't even the sort of business she'd expect to draw the attention of any self-respecting burglar...

But if she was wrong about that...there she stood, spotlighted in the hallway.

She dived for the switch to kill the lights. Her eyes were

slow to readjust to the dimness, and she'd managed to convince herself that she'd been startled by the movement of a tree branch in the breeze when a face pressed against the glass. The bevels distorted the image, so it wasn't her eyes so much as the way her stomach tightened which told Alison who was outside. She unlocked the door, pulled it open, and looked up at Logan Kavanaugh.

"So you *are* here," he said. "I saw lights on in the basement and then that sudden flash up here, and I suspected it would be you."

"Congratulations. Does finding me make you eligible for a prize?" She didn't move aside.

"Are you going to invite me in?"

"Any reason I should? Business hours are—"

"Looks to me like your business hours are about like mine—whatever it takes to get the job done."

He did look tired, she thought. There was a network of fine lines around his eyes. She stepped back from the door. "Would you like a cup of coffee?"

"If it's already made."

"It won't take a minute. Believe me, you don't want to drink the tar that's left in the pot."

Logan shrugged. "I've no doubt had worse." He followed her down the stairs and into the big kitchen next to her office.

Alison dumped the glass carafe, rinsed it, and started a fresh pot brewing. "So what brings you here?" She didn't look at him. "No, don't tell me. I bet you're so shaken at being done with work at this hour—my goodness, it's only eight o'clock!—that you've decided to take me on as a patient after all."

"This was supposed to be my afternoon off," he said gloomily. "If I was out beating the bushes for anything, it'd be a doctor—we're short one just now." He shook his head at the sugar bowl she held up. "I thought perhaps you'd decided on another approach to your problem, since you haven't called for a referral.''

Alison set a steaming cup in front of him. "I'm amazed, with all those rafts of patients to see, that you'd bother to keep track of me.''

He grinned, and the tired lines around his eyes crinkled with humor. "Purely in self-defense, I assure you. Though as a matter of fact, I didn't know till today that you hadn't called.''

Alison poured her own coffee and sat down across from him. "So what was special about today?''

"This came in the mail.'' He reached into the inside breast pocket of his jacket and pulled out an envelope. "I don't suppose you know anything about it.''

His tone, Alison thought, said that he'd already convinced himself differently.

She looked warily at the envelope. The return address was Tryad's, the envelope identical to the ones they had printed by the thousands. Logan's name and office address had been neatly typed. She turned it over, looked up at him, and shook her head. "I can't imagine why you think I'd be sending—''

"Go ahead, open it.''

"The cloak-and-dagger way you're acting, I'm not sure I want to leave my fingerprints,'' she muttered, but she slid the contents out. She recognized the long, narrow card immediately; it was one of the elegant gift certificates she'd produced, good for one year's membership in the Chicago Singles.

She tried without much success to choke back a laugh. *Susannah,* she thought, *the little matchmaker!* The whole notion of gift certificates had been Susannah's; Alison should have seen this coming. "And you thought I'd enrolled you? No, I can't take credit for that. Lucky you. It's a pretty pricey gift, you know.''

"*Can't* take credit? Or *won't?*"

"I had nothing to do with it. I have to admit I have my suspicions about who's responsible, but—"

"It's your signature, Alison."

"Of course it is. I signed a whole stack of blanks, but they're not valid till Rita numbers and registers them. She no doubt has a record of who paid the bill. If you like, I'll ask her tomorrow. I can also—"

"It's a shame, you know. I was so certain it was you I brought you a gift in return." From the other inside breast pocket, he took a small, flat white box and set it down on the table beside his cup.

"Very thoughtful," Alison said dryly. "But I still don't quite understand why you'd think that *I*—"

"Because the whole idea sounds like one of your fruitcake plans—and when I found out you hadn't pursued the medical alternative, it all fit with your twisted logic. What better way to meet a transient population of males than to set up your very own singles club?"

Alison shook her head in confusion. "So I can look over the selection and choose one to father my baby? Oh, please. Even if I was crazy enough to do that, why would I let you in on it?"

"In the hope that I'd feel so bad about the risks you'd be taking that I'd volunteer to help after all."

"You'd be more likely to issue a general warning in the name of protecting your fellow men." She tapped the heavy vellum gift certificate on her palm. "I'll give this back to Rita tomorrow and have her issue you a refund check."

"Didn't your mother ever tell you it isn't polite to return a gift for the money?"

"As a matter of fact," Alison said dryly, "no, she didn't."

Logan extracted the gift certificate from her hand and put

it gently back into his breast pocket. "Besides, someone obviously thought I'd find this fun—and who knows? They might just be right. And the least I can do is stand by to give—what did you call it? A general warning to protect my fellow men, wasn't that it? Thanks for the coffee." With a theatrical sweep, he bowed and was gone, leaving Alison sitting with cup in hand staring at nothingness.

Finally she shook her head a little and smiled. Let the man have his joke. He wouldn't show up within miles of the Chicago Singles; he just wanted her to think he might.

She stood up and started to clear the table. Only when she picked up his cup did she realize that he'd gone off without the small, flat box.

I was so certain it was you I brought you a gift in return, he'd said.

If the box had been sealed or wrapped, she wouldn't have opened it. But it was neither, and it would have taken a lot more willpower than Alison possessed to keep from lifting the lid and peeking inside. She wasn't hurting anything, after all. He'd never even know she'd looked.

On a bed of white cotton lay a silver pin just a couple of inches tall, in the shape of a musician with a flute raised to his lips. The workmanship was delicate, the most beautiful Alison had ever seen. And what instinct had told him that the flute was the instrument she'd always wanted to play?

Her fingertip went out hesitantly. The silver warmed instantly to her touch, and—almost frightened by the pleasure which swelled her heart—she snapped the lid back on the box and put it in the drawer of her desk, where it would be safe till she could send it back to him.

CHAPTER THREE

ALISON ticked items off the list in her head as she laid them out on her desk. Membership booklets to hand out at the Chicago Singles meeting, application forms for those who hadn't already formally signed up, receipts in case anyone wanted to pay dues, notes for her brief introductory talk...

She reached for her soft leather briefcase and began to pack it. The back door banged and heels clicked on the bare wooden steps from the main floor down to Alison's office.

"Nice little black dress," Susannah said as she came in.

"Thanks. It's not what I'd normally wear to the art museum on a Saturday afternoon, but I won't have time to change before the Singles meeting."

"I'm glad you're not still calling it the Stupid Singles." Susannah flung herself down on the wicker couch. "You know, I surmise you're going to enjoy this club a whole lot more than you expect to."

I'll just bet you think so, Alison thought, *because you don't realize that I know about Logan's gift certificate!* The comment was the final confirmation of her suspicions that Susannah had been the source of that gift; she sounded entirely too innocent.

"Don't get me started," Alison said. "Sorry I'm not ready, by the way. It took longer to get everything together than I'd planned. I could have met you at the museum— there was no need for you to go out of your way to pick me up here."

"Oh, no. I asked you to provide moral support, and I'm

43

going to squeeze out every drop of it I can—which includes having you walk into the Dearborn with me.''

Alison put the last of her papers in place and picked up the flat white box which contained the tiny flute player. Though she didn't for a minute expect that Logan would show up at the meeting tonight, she might as well be prepared; she'd drop the box into the side pocket of her briefcase just in case.

The lid slipped, and the pin tumbled from its bed of white cotton onto the slick surface of Alison's desk. Susannah swung around. ''What a luscious pin! You're going to wear it, aren't you? It was made for that dress.''

''Don't you think it's a bit much for the museum?'' The excuse was feeble, Alison knew, but it was all she could think of.

Susannah's eyebrows rose. ''Obviously you haven't been there for a while, or you'd know that anything goes. It's perfect. Want me to help you put it on?''

Great, Alison thought. *Now I have to start explaining how it's not really mine, it's sort of a gift from Logan, but I'm giving it back...and won't Susannah have a field day with that?*

There wasn't much choice except to explain—and Susannah wouldn't be easily put off with less than the full story. Unless...she *could* just wear the thing. What would be the harm? The pin certainly wouldn't be injured, and if she took it off the minute she was out of Susannah's sight, Logan would never know it had been out of the box.

Coward, she told herself. But she handed Susannah the small silver figure and stood very still while it was fastened to the shoulder of her dress.

It was apparent the moment they stepped into the Dearborn Museum of Art that everyone knew the famous artist would be inspecting the damage to his work that afternoon, for the museum was as busy as Alison had ever seen it. Most of the crowd was gathered in the main gallery where the damaged painting was, to Alison's surprise, still hanging. Few of them were looking seriously at the art, and when Susannah and Alison came in, the noise level dropped and all eyes focused on them.

On Susannah, rather. Alison knew very well that no one was paying any particular attention to her. Still, as they walked up the wide ramp into the main gallery, she felt as if every gaze in the museum was directed at the small silver flute player on her shoulder.

Guilt, she told herself, *is a powerful thing.*

"Perfect timing," Susannah murmured, and just as Alison started to ask what she meant, the double doors at the back of the gallery opened and two men—the museum's director and a Bohemian figure who could only be the famous artist—strolled in and straight across the gray-carpeted floor to the painting in question.

The Bohemian's hand went to his heart as if he'd been stabbed. "The sin of it," he said, and a sympathetic murmur ran through the crowd.

Alison took a good look at the canvas. Then she tilted her head to one side and looked again. She couldn't see, herself, that the streak of green spray paint had done any particular harm to what she thought must be the most boring piece of art in the whole museum.

The crowd milled around the artist, offering their condolences. Susannah began to circulate, greeting the members of the museum board. Alison stayed close to her, on guard and ready to change the subject, but when it became obvious that Susannah was doing just fine on her own— exactly as Alison had expected—her attention began to wander.

The artist was surrounded, but she spotted the museum's director standing at the edge of the crowd, momentarily alone, and she strolled over to him. Now was as good a time as any to ask him about the Dearborn hosting some sort of event for the Chicago Singles. "Pierce, if you have a couple of minutes…"

The director turned. He looked stressed-out, Alison thought, but his suit was as precisely pressed as ever and his blond hair looked as if he'd painted it in place. "Oh, hello, Alison. What do you need?" His gaze strayed from her face down the lines of her dress, and paused.

"I'm getting the new singles group off the ground, but so far all the activities seem to center around food. I was wondering if…" She paused. Was he studying the silver pin or her anatomy? It wasn't like Pierce to be crude, and yet—

Pierce's gaze lifted momentarily to her face. "Yes?"

"If we could set up a special museum tour or… Pierce, is there something wrong?"

"Hmm? Oh, nothing, nothing. Just looking at your pin."

Alison's fingertips went automatically to the flute player. "It's unique, isn't it?"

Pierce cleared his throat. "Certainly very unusual. One doesn't often see these worn so prominently."

But how else, Alison wondered, would someone wear a pin? Not fastened to her underwear, that was sure; the whole point of jewelry was to be seen. *One doesn't often see these worn so prominently…* Pierce made her simple silver pin sound positively off-color. "What's wrong with it?" she asked suspiciously.

"Nothing at all. It's perfectly legitimate. Lovely Native American design, very well executed. No doubt, judging by the fine detailing, it's sterling silver."

"Then what—" She stopped, abruptly aware that the noise of the crowd around her had died down and her voice was louder than she'd realized.

Pierce didn't seem to notice the change. His words boomed out across the gallery. "But you do realize, don't you, dear girl, that the humpbacked flute player is a fertility charm?''

She was going to kill Logan Kavanaugh.

A fertility charm! And here she'd thought he was being so sweet to think of her, to shop for her, to look for something she'd particularly like.

She should have known he wouldn't have spent precious time hunting down an ordinary gift. She should have known anything that came from him would have a diabolical twist.

Well, she'd show him. She'd hunt him up, ram one silver flute player down his throat, and stand by to prevent anyone from using the Heimlich maneuver to remove it.

Of course, if she reacted so strongly, he'd know how very successful he'd been at embarrassing her. If there was anything she didn't want to do, it was to increase his pleasure in making a joke at her expense. Maybe it would be more effective to ignore the trick altogether while she quietly plotted a proper payback.

Ignoring him—yes, that was the ticket. She'd pretend that she'd never opened the box at all, that she was blithely unaware of the loaded meaning of the object inside. That would take the wind out of his sails—and more importantly it would discourage him from doing anything similar in the future.

In the unlikely case that they had a future.

She leaned forward in the cab to peer at the awning over the door of Coq Au Vin, one of Chicago's finest restaurants. ''They've changed the front entrance since I was here last,'' she said.

''According to my customers, that's not all they've changed,'' the cabbie muttered. He maneuvered as close to the awning as he could, and Alison handed over the fare and stepped out into the crispness of a mid-September evening.

The restaurant had been one of Chicago's premiere dining spots for more than a decade, catering to an elite and exclusive crowd, but Alison hadn't been inside since a new owner had taken over, renovated the whole place, and made a push to draw in new customers.

That change of focus was what made the partnership between Coq Au Vin and Chicago Singles a natural. Not only would the club's twice-monthly dinner meetings bring in several dozen diners—people who might well have been eating Chinese at home instead—but they were exactly the sort of customer that the new Coq Au Vin was trying to attract. Young, single, professional, with money to spare...

Not that it looked as if the restaurant needed help, Alison thought. She almost had to push her way through the lobby to the reservations desk, and when she got there the maître d' looked a bit frazzled.

She'd allowed herself an extra half hour before the time set for the first gathering of the Chicago Singles, in order to check out the arrangements she'd ordered and do her last-minute preparations. But by the time Alison got the maître d's attention, her time cushion was almost gone. When, instead of taking her to the dining room set aside for the club, he went off to find the owner—who, he said, had insisted on doing the honors himself—Alison was left biting her tongue.

"I wouldn't worry about it," a soft voice said from well above her left shoulder. "With this crowd, you're not the only one who'll be late."

She spun around and looked up into Logan Kavanaugh's deep green eyes. In the dim lobby, they were even more striking; the soft light from the wall sconces caressed his lashes, casting long shadows across his face. It also emphasized the small white line on his lower lip—the scar she'd left on him in their first encounter.

No doubt, she thought, *some women would find that sexy.*

"Why couldn't I be lucky enough that you were one of the late ones?" she muttered.

The maître d' had returned. "May I help you, sir?"

"Oh, no," Logan said cheerfully. "I'm just one of Ms. Novak's strays. Sorry—singles." He glanced down at her. "You look surprised to see me. Didn't I tell you I was coming?"

"You threatened something of the sort. Though I'm amazed you actually managed to get away from your patients long enough to come."

He pushed back his jacket, and she saw a tiny pager clipped to his belt. "There's no guarantee it'll last, of course."

"I'll keep my fingers crossed," Alison said sweetly.

He grinned. "I'd ask which way you're hoping for, but I suspect I already know. Nice dress, Alison. Awfully plain, though, isn't it?"

Alison glared at him. Her fingertips slid to the flat white box in the side pocket of her briefcase, and then let it drop. If she handed the flute player back now—acknowledging that his transparent comment had reminded her of the pin—she might as well take out a full-page ad announcing that she'd peeked.

"Ms. Novak?" A tall tuxedo-clad man appeared beside her and offered his arm. "Welcome to Coq Au Vin. I'm Jason Lee, the new owner. Let me show you to the room we've reserved."

Logan followed her so closely that Alison swore she could feel the gold buttons of his blazer through the back of her dress. But before she could decide whether to keep on ignoring him or take a half step back and squash his foot, Jason Lee had flung open the door of a private dining room.

Tables for six were set up around the perimeter of the room, far enough apart to let each group enjoy a private conversation but close enough that the room felt warm and inviting. The center of the room had been left empty so the whole group could mix before and after the meal.

"This is great," Alison said. "Just what I asked for."

With a theatrical bow, the owner excused himself to tend to his other guests.

Logan looked around the room. "We could dance," he suggested, "while we're killing time waiting for everyone else."

"Go right ahead." Alison laid her briefcase on an extra table near the door and started to unload it. "I have things to do."

"Oh, in that case I'll help."

She didn't look up. "Good. Go wait by the front door, ask anyone who comes in alone if they're here for the Singles, and point them this direction. And by the way—" She pulled the flat white box from her briefcase. "You left this the other night."

Logan made no move to take the box. "Hang on to it for me, would you?"

There wasn't so much as a flicker of surprise—or even curiosity—in his face. Alison had to admit to feeling disappointed; she'd hoped he'd protest, trying to talk her into keeping the gift—or that he'd at least look startled. "Why? I certainly wouldn't want to forget to give it back to you."

"Because it'll spoil the nice lines of my jacket if I shove it in a pocket."

"You didn't worry about that last time you were carrying it around."

"But that wasn't a new jacket, and I wasn't trying to impress a roomful of women."

You certainly weren't trying to impress me, Alison thought. "It won't be just women tonight, you know. And Chicago Singles isn't a dating service. It was never intended for matchmaking purposes—it's more like a networking club. A place where people with similar interests can form friendships. A place to make business connections and find mentors. A place to meet people who'll cheerfully go along to the inevitable business banquets where they serve up rubbery chicken and limp green beans—''

''Impossible,'' Logan interrupted. ''Those people don't exist.''

''A place to find out about the best car repair shops—''

He began to applaud, each hand clap deliberate and distinct. ''Excuse me for a moment while I step out to get you a soapbox.''

Alison didn't pause. ''—Or to ask which doctors are best in their field.''

Logan looked vaguely interested. ''And which ones aren't? Watch out, Alison—that could be interpreted as a threat.''

''No,'' she said with mock horror. ''Could it, really? Tell me the name of your practice, again.''

''*Again?* I didn't think I ever had.''

She could hardly admit to hearing the title when she'd called his office, so Alison improvised. ''Kit told me.''

''Of course. It's Obstetrics and Gynecology Associates.''

''That sounds even worse than the first time I heard it. You know, somebody ought to consider improving that name.''

''Why? It's perfectly accurate and descriptive.''

''It's a tongue twister. And not only that, a patient could die of old age while she's waiting for the receptionist to finish saying it.''

''What would you suggest instead?''

Alison stopped arranging membership handbooks and looked up at him through her lashes. ''If you want me to give it some thought, I'll be happy to write up Tryad's standard memo of agreement for services to be rendered.''

''With not even a free sample? Alison, my dear—''

"Do *you* give free samples of medical care?"

"Absolutely. You haven't gotten a bill from me yet, have you?" He put a finger to his lip and added thoughtfully, "The fact that my reason for not sending a bill is that I'm trying to forget the occasion is entirely beside the point."

She might have given him another scar, if a couple of lost-looking young women hadn't wandered in just then, and she had to get down to business.

For a man who'd indicated interest in *a roomful of women*, Logan Kavanaugh seemed singularly shy. He was hardly ever more than three feet from Alison. Twice during the evening, she actually stepped on him; the second time she turned around and said in exasperation, "I don't have laryngitis, Logan. If I need you, I can still raise my voice and call. Though why on earth I would need you…"

After that he stayed a little farther away, and whenever she glanced his direction he seemed to be surrounded by femininity and having a very good time. But when the meeting broke up, the final questions were answered, and the last two women reluctantly left the restaurant. Logan was still there. He was leaning against the wall near the door, arms folded across his chest, eyes closed. His breathing was so regular Alison wondered if he was asleep.

She started to gather up the leftover handbooks and application forms. "Something on your mind, Kavanaugh?"

He stirred and opened his eyes. "Tell me again about how this isn't a dating service. You could have fooled me—I got at least a dozen invitations."

"Lucky you. In that case, I guess you're not wondering whether you can still turn in your membership."

"You'd let me?"

She was surprised to find that her reaction wasn't relief that he still wanted to, but something closer to puzzlement. Why would he give up that kind of popular success? "Of course. There's no point in having members who aren't enthusiastic.''

He said something under his breath which Alison didn't catch. She zipped her briefcase and tucked it under her arm.

Logan pushed himself away from the wall. "Come on, I'll take you home."

"I don't need a ride."

"Of course you do. I saw you arrive in a taxi. Besides, I'm afraid the last two women who left may be waiting outside to ambush me."

"Poor darling," Alison mocked. "Perhaps you *should* turn in your membership, if it's going to cause problems."

"Why did you think I was trying to stay close to you?" he said. "For protection, that's why."

Alison thought he was trying very hard to sound pathetic—without a lot of success, in her opinion. "Oh, I wasn't worried about you," she said sweetly. "I was thinking of the good of the club. If you often suffer delusions like this about your overwhelming attractiveness—"

He angled an assessing look down at her, then took her elbow and walked her toward the door. "For that, I should make you take a cab. Have you found out any more about that gift certificate?"

Alison shook her head. "It was paid for with cash. Rita said it came in the mail—an envelope full of twenties, wrapped in a plain sheet of paper with your name and address typed on it. That's all. So she filled out the certificate and mailed it."

"It's hardly fair of whoever it was," he murmured, "not to let me know who to thank for the good time."

"Or who to get even with?"

"Something like that."

Alison tried not to smile. "It could just as easily have been you," she murmured. "Not wanting to admit that it was your idea to join." Though as a matter of fact, Alison was still certain that Susannah was at the bottom of it, and that she'd gone to such lengths not because she was hiding from Logan but because she didn't want her partner to know what she'd done. At any rate, whatever Susannah's reasons, loyalty to her kept Alison silent.

Plus, she told herself, why give Logan the pleasure of getting even, when she herself would so enjoy paying Susannah back?

Alison hurried down State Street, umbrella dripping. It was impossible to dodge the puddles; each step splashed cold rainwater halfway to her knees. Most of the time the cold trickle was merely unpleasant, but at each cross street, the breeze coming west from the lake seized raindrops and turned them into razor blades slicing at her skin.

Autumn rain was the nastiest kind, she'd always thought. Spring showers could be just as cold and bleak, but at least they held the promise of warmth, freshness, and renewal just ahead. September rains only promised to lead to winter.

She tipped her umbrella up a bit as she reached the intersection, trying to spot a cab. A passing car struck a larger-than-usual puddle, sending a wave of muddy water toward Alison. She leaped back, avoiding the wave that would have been the absolute end of her new black pumps. But the brown paper bag she carried tipped, spilling the top layer of peaches onto the sidewalk, and this time Alison couldn't dodge fast enough. The overripe fruit hit concrete with the same explosion as would a soft snowball, and peach pulp dotted not only her new shoes, but her sheer black stockings and the hem of her wool tweed skirt.

She glared at the mess and considered dropping the bag—now only half full—into the nearest waste can, but just then an empty cab pulled alongside and she ran for it, waving madly.

By the time the cabbie delivered her to Tryad's brownstone, she'd used a whole packet of tissues and gotten most of the peach pulp cleaned off. The remainder would require a long hot soak; it was beginning to dry into the fibers of her skirt and stockings. She growled a little and asked the cabbie if he could use a bag of peaches.

"Is that what I smell back there?" he said, and from the tone of his voice Alison concluded he wasn't much of a fruit eater. She paid the fare, gathered up her peaches, opened her umbrella once more and splashed up to the brownstone.

Susannah was sitting on the corner of Rita's desk, the telephone to her ear. "As soon as possible, thanks." She put it down and looked doubtfully at Alison. "I was beginning to wonder if you were going to make it back. You look a little the worse for wear, you know."

"Chicago cabbies are the best weather predictors in the world. Half an hour before it starts to rain, they all disappear. It's some kind of law." Alison snapped her umbrella shut and stood it in a corner to dry. "Where's Rita?"

"I sent her home. The furnace has apparently gone on the blink since we used it last spring—at least, when I tried to turn it on, it produced very strange noises instead of heat. And since Rita's already nursing a cold, I figure the last thing she needs is a chill." She sniffed. "What's in the bag?"

"Peaches." Alison set the bag on Rita's desk and kicked off her shoes. "They were a bargain." *Of course,* she thought, *by the time I get the pulp cleaned out of my suit, the deal won't be so cheap.*

With a cautious fingertip, Susannah pulled the bag open and glanced in. "Are you sure they were a bargain? I'll bet you just felt sorry for the street vendor."

Alison shrugged, and then shivered. "All right, she looked cold. Just like me. Was that the furnace repair people you were calling?"

"Of course. They'll be along sometime this century—if we're lucky. In the meantime, if you want to get warm, I've got just the ticket for you."

Susannah's voice held the airy note which Alison had long ago learned to suspect.

"A new client," Susannah went on. "You're going to love this. That sultry-voiced receptionist in Logan Kavanaugh's medical practice called this afternoon. The doctors want to talk to a PR person."

"What's to love about *that?* And why me?"

Susannah shrugged. "Maybe they're going to change that frightful name. And it has to be you. Since Kit's a patient, she has a conflict of interest."

And I don't? Alison almost said. She managed to swallow the words; wouldn't Susannah enjoy interpreting that? "What about you?"

"But, darling, I can't leave the office now. I'm the only one who can describe the strange noises the furnace made. And the doctors want someone as soon as possible."

"Figures," Alison grumbled. "They keep everybody else waiting forever, but when they want something...."

"I told them you'd be there at half past five."

Alison glanced automatically at her wristwatch. "I hope it doesn't take long. I have a date."

Susannah's eyes sparkled. "A real live one?"

"Rob changed the tickets for *Rigoletto* so I could go."

"Oh. Just one of your pals, then. Well, at least you can get nice and warm in the meantime, lucky girl. With all the half-naked patients, doctors' offices have to keep the heat turned up." Susannah gave an artistic shiver. "You aren't planning to leave these peaches here, are you?"

Alison stepped into her shoes and picked up the bag. "Consider yourself lucky I'm not pelting you with them. First the gift certificate, and now this—"

"What gift certificate?"

"The one you bought for Logan's membership in the Chicago Singles."

Susannah looked blank.

"The gift certificates themselves were your idea, Sue. Don't play innocent with me."

"I'm not playing," Susannah said. "I *am* innocent. Somebody enrolled Logan in your singles club?" She snickered. "See? I told you you'd have fun before this was over!"

The rain had stopped, and from the front porch Alison could hear Mrs. Holcomb muttering next door as she swept water off her steps. Inspiration struck, and Alison dashed down to the sidewalk and around to Mrs. Holcomb's side.

The woman had no time to retreat; instead, she seemed to freeze in place, slightly crouched, broom at the ready. It was the best view Alison had ever gotten of Mrs. Holcomb. Her face was pale and as lined as a spider web, and her dark eyes were narrowed with apprehension.

Alison held out the bag. "I'd like to give you these peaches, Mrs. Holcomb, if you can use them."

For a moment she thought the woman hadn't heard, and then one withered hand stretched out toward the bag. "Peaches?"

"They're extremely ripe, I'm afraid." Alison took a slow step forward. "Perhaps you won't want—"

Mrs. Holcomb's hand clutched the bag. "Can't waste them," she said. She looked at the fruit, and then up at Alison, and her eyes brimmed with tears. "It's very nice of you."

"I hope you'll enjoy them," Alison managed to say. She retreated, feeling thoroughly ashamed of herself. It was uncomfortable to be looked on as a benefactor when in truth she hadn't been doing a good deed, just ridding herself of a nuisance. But at least Mrs. Holcomb would have some fresh fruit today; Alison had often wondered what the woman ate and where she got it. None of them had ever seen her venture out to the store.

Susannah had written down not only the address of Logan's medical practice but precise directions for getting there. Obstetrics and Gynecology Associates occupied an entire floor of a building devoted to medical offices, and it was obviously not only a big practice but a lucrative one. The waiting room was comfortably and stylishly furnished, and though the art on the walls was probably not the caliber of what she'd seen at the Dearborn Museum last week, it didn't take a professional to tell it was good quality.

Besides, Alison thought, she liked it better than what the museum considered art. There was one piece, an impressionistic painting of a mother nursing an infant, which reached down into her heart and tugged as all her own longing for a child swept over her once more.

But there was no time to stare at paintings, or to think of babies. She was right on time; though she'd hoped to have a few quiet minutes to think before confronting Logan and his partners, she didn't have that luxury. And though they surely couldn't expect any kind of organized presentation in this first meeting, Alison prided herself on being as prepared as possible. It would have been nice to have a couple of new names ready, especially since Logan had had a couple of days to think over her suggestion and discuss it with his fellow doctors.

The receptionist looked up from the telephone and smiled. "Sorry to keep you waiting. You're here to see…?"

"Dr. Kavanaugh," Alison said, and gave her name.

The receptionist pushed a button on the console in front of her. "Dr. K., Ms. Novak is here to see you."

There was a brief pause and an answer which sounded like gibberish to Alison. The receptionist obviously understood it, however, for she released the button and said,

"Dr. K.'s office is the farthest back on the main corridor. It winds a bit, but if you keep bearing right, you'll get there."

The waiting room had been open and airy, but behind the scenes the offices and examining rooms formed a maze worthy of a laboratory rat. *And the rat would probably do better at getting through,* Alison thought. *A mere person could wander around for a decade.*

Most of the rooms were empty, with doors standing open, but a few were closed off as if still in use; she supposed the last of the day's patients were inside, waiting to be seen. She wondered if they'd ever misplaced anyone…

She was starting to feel as if she was going around in circles when she heard a conversation somewhere ahead of her.

"—A narrow line here," said a man's brusque voice. "Men in this field are always subject to extra scrutiny, and now that we've had this incident with Templeton—"

"I'm not Templeton."

That, surely, was Logan's voice, Alison thought, and she picked up her pace. Ahead, the corridor seemed to widen into a secondary lobby of sorts, and that must be where the voices were coming from.

The brusque man went on, "It's still a potential problem. We've already had one man's conduct sour things for the whole practice. We're going to be under close scrutiny as it is."

Puzzled by the tone of the exchange, Alison started to draw back, but it was too late. She was already into the last bend of the corridor, and the two men had heard her. The brusque-sounding one wheeled around. He looked, Alison thought, as if he were about to yell at someone. She just hoped it wasn't her; she hadn't been purposely eavesdropping.

A couple of steps beyond him was Logan. His hands

were buried in the pockets of a long white lab coat; Alison couldn't help noting that the shapeless garment somehow made him look taller and stronger, while the older man's white coat just made him appear bulky.

"Excuse me," Alison said. "I didn't mean to intrude. I'm here because—"

Logan moved silently and swiftly, and before she could finish her sentence his hand was on her arm and he was drawing her forward. "Let me introduce you to Dr. Sinclair, Alison," he said. "Our senior partner."

"A pleasure, I'm sure." The man's gaze flicked across Alison and returned to Logan. "We'll talk about it again tomorrow, but don't expect me to change my mind. We can't take any more chances."

"You won't be taking a chance," Logan said. "And this young woman is why."

Alison's head was spinning.

"I still think you're wrong, Burt," Logan went on, "to think that Templeton was behaving inappropriately simply because he was single, and therefore all single men are suspect. But it's a moot point in my case. Burt, this is Alison Novak. She's going to be my wife."

Alison's knees turned to library paste; if it hadn't been for Logan's grip on her elbow she might have done a swan dive onto the hard tile floor.

She stared up at him. Logan smiled, and said, "And she's already told me she can't wait to start a family."

CHAPTER FOUR

ALISON could actually feel her eyes crossing with the shock. Suddenly there were two Logans, two Dr. Sinclairs, two corridors stretching endlessly before her…

I knew I wasn't very well prepared for this consultation, she thought, *but this is a new record. I came in to discuss a name change…only it's ending up to be* my *name we're talking about…*

Logan had lost his mind, that much was clear. She tested her footing; her knees were still trembling, but she thought she could stand upright without leaning on him if she had to.

Logan obviously felt her starting to pull away, for he put an arm around her, drawing her close to his side. Alison thought the gesture probably looked like a fond hug. In fact, she felt as if she were strapped into a straitjacket.

Time out, she wanted to yell. *Wrong patient!*

"Please," Logan said into her ear. If Alison hadn't known better, she'd have thought he was begging. The very idea of the arrogant Doctor Kavanaugh being reduced to imploring made her feel slightly hysterical. She shook her head a little. "Dammit, Logan—"

He raised his voice a trifle. "Darling, I'm sorry. I know we agreed we weren't going to tell anyone except family for a little while, but the news simply slipped out." He shrugged. "I guess I'm just too proud to keep it secret."

His eyes weren't emerald anymore but hunter green, so dark that she could hardly tell the pupil from the iris. The intensity of his gaze shocked her back into full sensibility. Whatever he was up to, Logan had a reason—a reason good

61

enough, in his own mind at least, to justify this farce. Whether Alison would agree with his logic was another matter entirely.

I'll listen to him, Alison thought grimly, *and* then *I'll dissect him.*

"No harm done," she said, and smiled at the older man. "I'm sure Doctor Sinclair will keep the news to himself."

She could feel tension drain slowly from Logan's body. "Your timing was perfect, sweetheart," he said. "I just finished with my last patient, and I can do hospital rounds later. Our reservation at Cicero's is—oops, we'd better be going right this minute or they'll give our table away." He guided Alison even farther into the maze of offices and pushed open a door which led onto an open fire stairway.

Alison paused on the iron grate which formed the landing. A cool breeze brushed her face; the damp, chilly air helped a little to restore her equilibrium.

"Why are you stopping? It's the private entrance," Logan said. "My car's parked right at the bottom."

"My umbrella is in your waiting room."

"I'll buy you a new one." He took her arm. "Look, Burt will be coming out himself anytime now—and we have to talk."

Despite his grip on her elbow, Alison clapped both hands to her face and pretended astonishment. "Do you think so? Really? What on earth could we need to discuss?"

"For one thing, what you were doing in the office in the first place."

Alison forgot to be careful on the grating, and the heel of her shoe slipped through an opening. Only Logan's hand on her arm saved her from a twisted ankle at the least. Of course, since she wouldn't have been on the fire escape at all if it wasn't for him, her gratitude was mixed with annoyance—especially when she inspected the shoe. The sharp edge of the steel grating had sliced the leather off the heel as efficiently as a carpenter's plane. "You can just return the umbrella," she said with a touch of acid. "But I'm sending you the bill for replacing the shoes. And what do you mean, what was I doing there? *Somebody* at Obstetrics and Gynecology Associates wanted to consult with a public relations person. I assumed it was you, about changing the stupid name."

"So that's it." Logan unlocked the passenger door of his car and helped her in. "I did say something to Burt the other day about the practice needing some PR, but I didn't think he took me seriously."

Alison tapped her fingertips on the leather upholstery while he walked around the car and got behind the wheel. "And he just happened to pick Tryad out of the phone book?"

"Oh, I probably mentioned the name, too. I was a little upset at the time, and I don't remember."

"Yeah? Well, if this is what you're like when you're upset, next time I'm running for cover."

"This? Oh, I'm not upset."

"What a relief," Alison said tartly.

Logan gave her a crooked grin. "Look, I'll explain it all. If you don't want to go to Cicero's—"

"Do you really have a reservation?"

"Of course not. But it's early yet."

"It's always noisy, though," she warned.

"That's the beauty of it. Everybody's talking so loud they don't bother to listen to anyone else."

"Well, you're the one who'll be talking, so if you don't mind screaming your personal business at the top of your lungs, it doesn't matter to me. At least it's close by. I can't stand this suspense much longer. What in heaven's name you were thinking of—"

Logan cut across two lanes of traffic to head toward downtown. A few minutes later, he turned the car over to the valet in front of Cicero's, in the heart of the Loop, and helped Alison out.

It might still be early for Chicago's diners, but the restaurant was already noisy and full of the wonderful aromas of Italian spices and sauces. A short, rotund man in a white apron hurried toward them. "Doc! Table for two? This way, please. It's been a while since we saw you. Busy with the babies and their mamas, eh?" He didn't wait for an answer before leading them through a series of dining rooms; eventually he stopped by a small round table in the most private, secluded corner Alison had ever seen. There were no chairs, only a rounded banquette couch just big enough for two, upholstered in dark red leather. If there had been a flashing neon sign above it announcing it was reserved for lovers, the message couldn't have been clearer.

"Your regular table?" she said dryly.

Logan smiled, but it was the restaurateur who answered. "No, no. The Doc, he never brings a lady. So now that he does, we make sure he has a nice table. That's all." He flourished menus at them and hurried away.

Alison shook her head in amazement and sat down, careful not to slide all the way around behind the table. The last thing she needed was for Logan to think she was encouraging him. "Do you suppose he expected me to believe that?" she mused. "*The Doc, he never brings a lady*—what a line. I never even knew this dining room was here. What kind of connections do you have to get this sort of treatment?"

"I delivered his latest—twin boys. Shall we have a bottle of wine?"

"I could use a little something for the shock, yes." Alison's tone was flippant but the words were true; her fingers were trembling almost uncontrollably as she shook out her napkin. Had Logan *really* announced their engagement just half an hour ago? And had she *really* not denied it and run screaming out of the building?

But the only other explanation was that she had been— and still was—hallucinating. Alison couldn't quite decide which would be worse.

The waiter brought a dusty bottle and two stemmed glasses. Logan tasted the wine and nodded; as soon as the waiter was gone, he lifted his glass. "To us," he said.

Alison shook her head. "Oh, no. Explanation first, and it had better be a good one. Then I'll decide what I'll drink to."

"It's a perfectly sensible arrangement, you know. And I'm not just thinking of me. It solves your problem rather neatly, too."

"*What?* You mean about a baby? How you managed to leap to that conclusion—" She couldn't go on. Was he seriously suggesting that *he* father her child? The idea didn't bear thinking about.

"I'll start at the beginning, shall I?" Logan swirled the wine in his glass and savored a mouthful till Alison was ready to scream. Then he sighed. "There are six of us in the practice. At least, there used to be."

She remembered something he'd said about being short a doctor just now. What that could have to do with his announcement was beyond her, but she wasn't about to interrupt for fear of slowing down the explanation even more.

"Dave Templeton left very suddenly about a month ago—not exactly by his own choice—after a patient complained about him."

Alison frowned. "One complaint? I'd think there are always going to be a few unhappy patients."

"There are—but one of this sort of complaint is enough." Logan's tone was dire. "He was sleeping with the patient."

"Oh." Alison could only begin to imagine the scenario. A patient who looked up to a doctor, who in turn took advantage of her... "The poor woman."

"Don't waste too much sympathy on her."

"What on earth are you talking about? He's the professional; it's his responsibility to keep things under control."

"You don't think I'm defending his behavior, do you?" Logan sounded annoyed. "You're absolutely right. He was entirely to blame. Personally, I'd like to see him lose his license, not just his job."

"Then I don't see—"

"But the patient was no innocent child. She didn't complain about the affair, she only reported him after it was over, to get even with him for dropping her. Otherwise, the odds are nobody would ever have known."

"And he'd have gone right on." Alison wasn't sure if she'd moved or Logan had, but she could feel the warmth of his body next to her. She shifted a little. "This is a fascinating discussion of medical ethics, Logan, but I don't quite see what it has to do with you—much less with me."

"Burt Sinclair went through the roof."

Alison frowned. "You were surprised?"

"By the way he's handling it, yes. He forced Templeton to resign with the excuse that he was ill, in order to keep as much strain as possible off the practice."

"Well, it might not be the best way to deal with—"

"No, it's not—but it's understandable to put out a cover story. There's going to be speculation. There always is when a doctor suddenly leaves a solid practice, especially if he isn't going straight on to something better. And the truth would put pressure on the rest of us. The whole practice would be watched more closely and any irregularity questioned."

"Even though none of the other doctors have done anything wrong?"

"Think about it. Having a bad apple as a partner is hardly the way to win trust from your patients—or your colleagues, either. At the very least they'll wonder whether everyone else in the practice knew about the crummy conduct."

"Knew, looked the other way, and only threw him out when he was obviously going to become a public embarrassment?" Alison nodded. "I see."

"Anyway, Burt thinks he can head off the questions before they're asked. That's probably why he wanted to talk to you." He frowned. "Though I can't imagine him actually confiding all this, or asking for advice when he thinks he's already got the problem solved."

"By doing what?" Alison said blankly.

"He's willing to go to any lengths and make any sacrifice to eliminate even the tiniest cause for scrutiny. And since Templeton was single—and so am I—he's fixed on me as a potential problem."

I'm not Templeton, she'd heard him tell Burt Sinclair. Now it made sense.

Alison was almost sputtering. "He thinks just because you're not married you'd do the same thing Templeton did? But that's ridiculous!"

Logan's eyes gleamed, but in the dimness of the isolated corner Alison couldn't interpret the sudden glow. "Thank you for your faith in me."

"That's not what I intended to say," she said irritably. "I mean... Sorry, that didn't come out right at all. I didn't plan to insult you, either. I was only saying that being married wouldn't have prevented Templeton from doing just as he liked."

"*You* know that," Logan said patiently. "And *I* know that. And I imagine Burt Sinclair will eventually come around to admitting it, too, when he regains his senses. In the meantime, however—"

"Are you telling me your job is hanging on this?"

"Exactly. Well, now that we have all that out of the way…" He set his glass down and looked around for the waiter. "Shall we order? The kitchen will be starting to get busy, and I do need to make hospital rounds sometime tonight."

Alison stared at him. Very carefully, she set her wineglass down and turned to face him directly. "Now wait a minute, Kavanaugh. You may have finished telling your story, but that's hardly the end of this discussion."

"So we'll eat while we talk," Logan said reasonably. He sniffed. "Do you smell peaches? It's the strangest thing, but ever since we came in here I'd swear I smell—"

"Forget the peaches," Alison ordered. "I want a few answers. For one thing, how long have you been considering this incredible notion? And did it ever occur to you to give me some warning?"

Logan considered. "Not long, and no. How could I? He hit me with his views just before you walked in. Until then, I didn't realize I was in any particular danger."

"So telling him you were getting married was a completely knee-jerk reaction?"

"I suppose you could say…" He broke off as the waiter came up to the table. "What would you like, Alison?"

"I don't care what I eat. I don't even care *if* I eat."

"Now that's no proper attitude—especially in a place like this. Luigi would be hurt." He murmured to the waiter, handed over the menu, and leaned back with an air of accomplishment. "Where were we?"

"Talking about your idiotic announcement. This is an insanely complex way to solve a problem, you know."

"It's not your garden variety problem."

"All right, I'll admit that. But it's doomed, Logan. It's

bound to fall apart. Nobody would believe we...that the two of us..." Her voice failed.

He was watching her with bright-eyed interest, but he didn't say a word.

Alison cleared her throat. "Why did you pick on me, anyway? Come to think of it, why did you have to give a name at all?"

"Do you think Burt would believe I couldn't remember who my fiancée is? And if I couldn't produce her in short order—"

"You could have dodged the question till the Singles meeting next weekend and talked to one of those twelve women you said were so interested in you. I'm sure at least one of them would volunteer."

Logan released a breath with a whoosh. "And you think *I* come up with complex ways to solve problems? Those women are serious trouble. Anyway, your being there seemed like fate. Burt brings up the whole sad business, and suddenly there you stand, like an answer to prayer. An angel, sent to help."

"Sorry I didn't know that in advance." Alison's voice was just short of sugary. "I'd have polished up my halo and pressed my wings."

Logan went on as if she hadn't spoken. "On the other hand, you were sort of my worst nightmare, too."

"Both at the same time? I had no idea I was so talented."

"It shook me up pretty badly when I saw you come in, you know. At first I thought you'd come about the baby again—"

"Right," Alison said dryly. "Like I didn't get the message the first time around."

"—And I was afraid you'd blurt out the details of that little discussion in front of Burt Sinclair. Right now would be an especially bad time for him to hear that little story. Then I realized perhaps that was the whole idea. Maybe your being there at that moment wasn't a coincidence. The whole question of you wanting help to have a baby was so incredibly odd—''

''Thank you very much.''

''—It occurred to me that perhaps it had been a setup. Maybe Burt had even hired you to check me out, see if I'd fall into the trap and suggest something unethical, so he could feel justified in firing me.''

Alison nodded. ''And I went to all the trouble of giving myself appendicitis just so I could meet you, too.'' Her voice rose. ''Are you seriously suggesting that I'd be involved in anything of the sort?''

''Well, you have to admit I had good reason to be a little disturbed just then. So maybe my judgment wasn't the best.''

''Your judgment,'' Alison said icily, ''would fit in a thimble with plenty of room left over.''

''I'm just telling you what was going through my mind. Anyway, the first thing I could think of was to undercut any accusation you might make. And maybe I could fend off Burt's argument at the same time. So I opened my mouth and the announcement just popped out.''

The waiter came back with salads and warm, crusty bread coated with olive oil and seasonings. Alison absentmindedly tore a chunk of bread into bits. ''I see why you thought that announcing your engagement would be the solution to all your problems,'' she said finally. ''Particularly since you didn't take the time to think it through. But you know, it's a very shortsighted approach. Just saying that you're getting married isn't going to fool anyone for long. And—''

Logan wasn't looking at her. He seemed to be intent on

the enormous olive he'd speared with his salad fork. "I'm not just saying I'm getting married."

"What?" Her voice was faint.

"I'm really getting married."

"Well, congratulations. I must admit I wish you'd used her name instead of dragging me into this, but I suppose there—" His emerald gaze focused on her, and Alison's voice trailed off. "Oh, no. It was bad enough when I thought you only wanted to masquerade as an engaged couple. But to actually *marry*.... No."

He simply looked at her.

"It's nothing personal, you understand," Alison said. "It's just that I'm never getting married, so I certainly don't plan—"

"Good." Logan's voice was brisk and businesslike. "I knew this was going to work out just fine." He pushed his salad plate aside and propped both elbows on the table. "Now we just have to settle the details…"

Alison was feeling desperate. "Are you having a problem with your ears? I just said I am *not*—"

"This is hardly like getting married."

"But you just said… You mean you're simply planning to take the charade one step farther than I thought? Instead of pretending to be engaged, you'll pretend to be married? What are you planning to do, stage a wedding that's actually a costume ball?"

Logan shook his head. "No, I'm afraid the marriage will have to be legal. It's just that it won't be *real*. Or at least, not long-lasting." He picked up his spoon and used the pointed handle to draw a series of parallel lines on the tablecloth. "I've been thinking. If you'll do this one little thing for me, Alison—"

She shook her head in disbelief. "*This one little thing?*

Getting married does not exactly fall under the heading of a simple favor, Kavanaugh.''

''—I'll make sure you end up with a baby.''

Alison closed her eyes, but it didn't help to stop her head from spinning, or suspicion from gnawing at her. ''And what precisely does that mean?''

''I thought it was perfectly plain English. I said—''

''You've said a lot of things on the subject. Like how I ought to try the old-fashioned way.''

''Well, it would be the easy—''

''So what you're really suggesting is that we have a short-term fling? What a charming idea—from your point of view. It would make the marriage look a whole lot more convincing, and you might even have some fun. Is that it?''

''That isn't exactly—''

''Because if so, that is not at all what I have in mind.''

''Of course not.'' Logan flung the spoon down as if it were a challenge. ''As I recall, you weren't suggesting any relationship as long or involved as a one-night stand, much less a short-term fling. What is it with you and men, anyway? Don't you have *any* normal instincts?''

She glared at him, but she was just as annoyed at herself as with him. She could have just said *No, thanks.* She didn't have to jump to conclusions and make a fool of herself.

Logan said coolly, ''I meant that whatever you want, I'll get for you. You want an anonymous donor, fine. In vitro? You've got it. Hell, I'll figure out a way to grow the kid entirely in the lab if you want, so you don't even have to deal with morning sickness and labor pains. All you have to do is go through a meaningless ceremony.''

Alison could hardly recognize her own voice. ''You're absolutely serious about this, aren't you?''

Logan flung his head back against the upholstered leather. ''Give the woman a prize.''

"Your job is that important to you?"

"You maybe don't need one yourself?"

She shook her head. "I was talking about this particular job. There must be plenty of others. Doctors are always in demand, aren't they? And you must be good—Kit would have checked that out before she came to you."

"Thank you," he said meekly. "Your confidence in me is quite humbling. Perhaps I should ask you to put that testimonial in writing."

"Knock it off, Kavanaugh. You could go to work anywhere. So what's the big deal about pleasing Burt Sinclair?"

"I'm not such a pitiful yes-man, if that's what you mean. But being forced out of the first position I've held as a fully qualified doctor wouldn't do my reputation any good."

Something he'd said earlier seemed to echo in her mind. "There's speculation when a doctor suddenly leaves a solid practice," she repeated slowly, "especially if he isn't going straight on to something better."

"Exactly. And if the truth about Templeton were to leak out…"

"Everyone would suspect you were guilty, too?"

"That's about the size of it. Under those circumstances, it might take a long while to find another situation."

"I can see your point. But surely you don't mean you're so scared that you actually want to continue to work with people who feel this way."

"Until today," Logan pointed out, "I didn't know they felt this way."

"And now that you do know?"

"My career plans changed in a hurry about thirty seconds after Burt Sinclair opened his mouth this afternoon. Or, to be more accurate, all my plans went out the window and left nothing much behind. There are practices that are a great deal more open-minded, and believe me I'm going to start looking. But I'd like to make that decision in my own time, and when I've had a chance to think it over and choose what I want. I don't want my choices limited by someone else's rotten behavior. And I don't want to have to make decisions which will affect my entire future under the extra pressure of being unemployed and falling behind in paying off my med school loans.''

Alison said slowly, ''And once you've found a new job?''

''Then it'll be goodbye Burt Sinclair.''

''I meant, what about the marriage?''

''Well, I won't need it anymore, will I?'' Logan asked reasonably. ''And since you never wanted it in the first place, I doubt we'd have too much trouble agreeing to divide the pots and pans.''

She sat silently for a few seconds. ''How long do you think it would take for you to find the job you want?''

''Six months—tops. Maybe a good deal less.''

Six months. That was all he was asking. If she invested six months—maybe a great deal less—she'd have her heart's desire.

''And you'll give me your word about...'' Her throat was so dry that her voice was nothing more than a raspy whisper. ''...The baby?''

Logan looked straight into her eyes. His own were dark, clear, almost somber. ''I promise.''

Alison was the first to blink. She looked away, put a trembling hand to her face, tried to concentrate. The whole suggestion was incredible. Foolish. Idiotic.

But it had been hard enough to tell *him* what she wanted, to pour out her reasons and defend her decision. She didn't want to start from scratch with another doctor who'd ask all the same questions, and still, perhaps, turn her away...

Logan didn't speak. He didn't move. But she knew he was still watching her just as intently, and waiting for her answer—a decision which would mean so much to both of them.

She toyed with the stem of her wineglass, and tried to steady her fingers as she picked it up and turned to him. ''Then I'll drink,'' she said huskily, ''to each of us getting what we want.''

Logan looked at her as if he hadn't heard, for a moment which stretched into eternity. Then he reached for his glass, and raised it to click against hers.

CHAPTER FIVE

WHEN Logan's car pulled up in front of Alison's row house, it was after nine o'clock. She hesitated for just a second as she unfastened her seat belt, not quite sure of the proper protocol. Should she invite him to come in with her? He wouldn't accept, of course; at least, she didn't think he would, since even though it wasn't late, he still had to stop at the hospital. And if she did ask him in, what should she offer? Not coffee, surely; the man had had at least four cups at Cicero's. She wondered, with that much caffeine in his blood, how he ever slept.

Logan shut off the engine and came around the car to help her out. *Well, that answers my question about inviting him,* Alison thought wryly.

"I'll walk you to the door," Logan said, "and wait till you're inside and have some lights turned on."

She bristled almost automatically. "I'm perfectly capable of getting myself safely into my own home."

"I'm certain you are," he said pleasantly, but he took her arm anyway, and Alison didn't fight it. The place *was* awfully dark tonight, now that he mentioned it. Normally she left lights on when she went out for the evening, but...

A car door slammed on the street, and a man's quick footsteps sounded on the pavement. Half consciously, Alison concluded that one of her neighbors was in a hurry to get inside. It wasn't until the steps approached her front door that she really began to pay attention, and then her heart speeded up. A dark night, a man following her...

Maybe she was glad Logan had insisted after all.

She fumbled with her keys and turned, ostensibly to

catch the moonlight which would help her identify the one which fit the front door, but actually to get a glimpse of the man who had followed them. Not as tall as Logan, his fair hair bright under the kiss of the moon...

"Rob," she said on a tiny breath of relief. "What are you doing here?"

Rob Morrow stopped less than three feet from them and planted his feet wide apart, his arms hanging easily at his sides. "Where the hell have you been, Alison?"

She said coolly, "Since when is it your business to check up on me?"

"When you make a date with me and don't show up."

Alison put two fingertips to the center of her forehead, where a tiny ache was quickly growing to earthquake proportions. She could hear herself telling Susannah, *I have a date... Rob changed the tickets for* Rigoletto... And then she had forgotten the opera entirely.

With good reason, of course. Logan Kavanaugh's spur-of-the-moment brainstorm would have made the Archbishop of Canterbury forget to say his bedtime prayers. But how she was going to explain *that* to a mad-as-a-wet-feline Rob Morrow...

"It's entirely my fault," Logan said.

Rob shifted his weight. "And just who are you?"

He looked as if he was about to take a swing at Logan, Alison thought, and he sounded just as threatening. She stepped forward, between the men.

She didn't quite know how it happened, but only a moment later she was once more neatly on the sidelines—in fact, she was standing almost behind Logan, who was facing Rob.

"Of course," Logan said easily, "I'm fairly sure it isn't every night that Alison receives a proposal of marriage— or at least that she accepts one—so I'm sure you understand why she's been a bit absentminded tonight about everything but me.'' He reached out to caress a lock of dark hair which had fallen over Alison's shoulder.

She shivered, and her pulse speeded up. It had been one thing for the two of them to talk about an engagement, but hearing the words out loud, addressed to someone else, seemed to make the whole situation more perilously real. Alison darted a look at Rob to see how he was taking the news.

He sounded as if the air had been let out of him. ''You're engaged? You're going to marry... I don't even know who he is, Alison!''

She introduced them. Logan shook hands and then turned back to Alison. ''Darling, you're tired. Do go in—I'll walk Mr. Morrow back to his car.'' Almost casually, he put an arm around her. ''Thank you for leaping to my defense, my dear. It was very sweet of you.''

She had only an instant's warning—the pressure of his hand against the small of her back, pulling her tightly against him—and she tipped her face up to his, ordering herself to look willing, even eager, for his kiss. She'd no doubt have to endure this from time to time, in order for the charade to be convincing. It was simply part of the cost of the bargain they had made.

His mouth against hers was gentle, but not at all tentative. An observer would think he'd kissed her dozens of times before—enough to know exactly how to fit her body, her lips, against his, but not enough to find the experience commonplace. And then he kissed her again, more hungrily. And again, pulling her even tighter against him, uttering a little groan, his tongue teasing...

Alison could hear her pulse beating against her eardrums; the man was sending her blood pressure through the roof. Her insides had turned to hot mush, and somehow her hands had crept up and linked at the nape of his neck...

''How touching,'' Rob said irritably.

Alison's body jerked taut. Logan didn't release her, but he did raise his head. "Oh," he said, sounding a bit blank. "Sorry, Morrow—I forgot you were there."

And if you believe that, Rob, Alison thought, *next he'll tell you that the Grand Canyon is only a ditch.*

Logan smiled down at her. "Goodbye, darling. I wish I could stay tonight. But perhaps if my rounds don't take too long…"

She had to admire how neatly he'd implied that he was a frequent overnight guest, and a more-than-welcome one. Of course, anyone who'd seen that kiss wouldn't be likely to feel doubt.

He nipped gently at her earlobe and whispered, "Good job. You were right on cue." He raised his voice. "There it is again—I told you I smelled peaches." He dropped a kiss on the bridge of her nose and turned to the other man, gesturing for Rob to precede him down the sidewalk.

Alison pushed the front door open and clutched the nearest solid object, the marble-topped table in the foyer. She was still reeling.

But only from the sheer unexpectedness of that embrace, she told herself, not because of the kiss itself. She'd been caught off guard, that was all, and this reaction wouldn't be repeated. Next time, she'd be prepared. She'd play along and make it look convincing, of course. But next time…

She sighed. Next time, she would *not* let herself forget that they had an audience.

Alison woke to a brilliant sunrise; the sky was streaked with pink and lavender and gold behind the deep steel blue of a few remaining clouds silhouetted against the brilliance. She sat up, dislodging a sleek black cat who'd been curled against the curve of her neck. He uttered a sleepy protest, and the other cat, a gray Persian mix, raised her head from the pillow on the opposite side of the bed, looking vaguely interested in the source of the noise. When she'd located and analyzed it, she yawned and curled up once more, putting a paw across her eyes.

"Ashes, I ought to get you a sleeping mask," Alison muttered. She pushed the blankets back and headed downstairs to the kitchen and the coffeemaker.

She felt as if she had a hangover, not from wine but from her dreams. She couldn't remember the details, but she had awakened abruptly in the middle of the night with the conviction that she couldn't go through with this, that first thing this morning she'd call Logan and tell him the deal was off.

Relieved, she'd sagged back into sleep and dreamed once more of the birthday party. There were two candles this time, and the child who waited none-too-patiently for the cake was definitely older, definitely a girl, her dark hair pulled up into a ponytail. Not a bad idea, Alison remembered thinking, in order to keep it out of the icing. She hadn't dropped the cake this time, but the dream had ended before she'd been able to place it in front of the eager child...

She caught the first stream of coffee in a mug, then shoved the carafe into place and wandered through the house, mug in hand, too restless to sit still.

Early morning sunshine filtered through the skylights set in the two-story-high cathedral ceiling, casting a soft glow over the enormous living room, turning the off-white walls to pale pink, and adding a bright gleam to the polished brass rail of the stair landing which formed a balcony just outside her bedroom. Beneath the balcony, at the back of the house, were the kitchen and guest room. Only the huge scale of the living room made them look small.

She paused at the door of the guest room—the room which one day soon might be a nursery. In her mind, she removed the antique oak bed, the matching dresser, the blanket chest, and substituted a white crib with a lacy frill, a changing table, a rocking chair. She stripped off the wallpaper with its subdued pattern—she'd always thought it looked like morning glory vines run wild—and put up stripes in red and blue and yellow against crisp white, with a border at toddler height of animals marching 'round and 'round the room.

She drank her coffee and considered. She couldn't make life-affecting decisions based on middle-of-the-night heebie-jeebies. And in the cool light of day, she knew she wasn't going to call Logan. She wouldn't back out. Nothing had changed since last night; this incredible deal of his was still her best opportunity to have the child she wanted so desperately. So what if she'd had a moment's apprehension about the whole idea?

She was feeding the cats when the doorbell rang. Frowning, she went to peek out the front window. Nobody ever dropped in on her at this hour. On the other hand, this wasn't an ordinary day; after the shock Rob Morrow had gotten last night, she could imagine him coming by to demand the details—or even organizing a vigilante group of her friends to find out what on earth was going on.

Logan was standing on the step, arms folded. As she watched he reached out to ring the bell again.

Impatient, aren't we? Alison thought. Then she realized that he didn't look impatient, simply very stern—and other possibilities started to hit her. Was *he* going to back out?

She told herself firmly not to jump to conclusions. There was no sense in feeling disappointed before she even knew what was going on...

Disappointed at not marrying him? she asked herself. But of course that wasn't it at all: he'd made a promise, and if that promise came to nothing, she'd be unhappy and disillusioned.

She pulled the door open just as his fingertip touched the

bell. "If you're feeling jangled this morning, it's probably because of all that coffee you drank last night."

"And good morning to you, too, Alison." He stepped inside. "Speaking of coffee, you wouldn't happen to have any, would you?"

She closed the door behind him. "I'd say that's the last thing you need." But she led the way to the kitchen nevertheless.

The two cats looked up only momentarily before concentrating once more on their breakfast. Alison poured coffee into a mug for Logan and refilled her own.

He was standing by the breakfast bar which—instead of a wall—separated kitchen from living room, and he was looking around with undisguised interest.

"Taking inventory?" Alison asked.

"All this light and air and modernness—somehow it doesn't seem like you."

"Really? Of course we've already established that you don't know me very well."

"But from the outside the house looks a hundred years old. Or does it seem that way because I've only seen it at night?"

"No, it's old. Originally it was a lot of tiny, dark, closed-in rooms, but the previous owner gutted the place and did this." She strolled back into the living room. "What brings you by so early, anyway?"

"Sorry about the hour, but the only time I can count on is before the day starts, and there were a couple of things we didn't talk about last night."

That at least didn't sound as if he'd changed his mind. She told herself it was silly to feel relieved; a woman with sense would be wary right now.

Alison pointed to a chair and perched on the arm of the matching couch. "Like what things?" she asked. "Because if you're planning to add conditions—"

"No, just make sure we both understand everything. For example, I don't think we made it absolutely clear that neither of us is allowed to confide the truth to anybody."

She laughed. "You mean I can't put up a billboard? Darn, and I was so looking forward to…" She realized how serious he looked. "Surely you don't think I *want* to share this scheme with anyone else?"

"I mean that not even Kit and what's-her-name—your other partner—can know the truth."

Alison said wryly, "And you expect me to have a problem with that? They're the ones I especially don't want to tell."

He looked curious, but he didn't ask. "And then there's a matter of a ring. I didn't even think of that till today."

"Oh. It hadn't occurred to me, either. But surely nobody will be too surprised if it takes a while. The way your schedule runs, you probably can't fit in another visit to a jeweler before Christmas."

He looked puzzled. *"Another?"*

Too late, Alison remembered that officially she'd never seen the silver flute player. She'd simply handed over the box the night he'd driven her home after the singles meeting, and—without comment—he'd tossed it into the back of the car. "Never mind. Slip of the tongue."

He let it pass. "Anyway, you're missing the point. This can't look like a brand-new engagement, or Burt Sinclair is going to be mighty suspicious. On the other hand, if we've been engaged for a while, you should already have a ring."

"You told him we were keeping it a secret," Alison pointed out. "I could hardly walk around Chicago in a diamond solitaire and not share the news."

"So you've been wearing it on a chain around your neck, nestled close to your heart."

"To keep the thought of you close to me. A sentiment

which is helped out every now and again when the chain twists and the prongs poke painfully into my skin.''

''Never mind. Now that the engagement's not a secret anymore, you can take it off the chain and put it on your finger.''

She put a hand to the center of her chest as if to feel for a ring. ''You know, Logan, you can tell a tall story so very well that you almost convinced *me* I was hauling a rock around my neck. So what do you have in mind? If you're saying you want me to go pick out an engagement ring on my lunch hour—''

She heard the catch in her voice, and she stopped in utter astonishment. *What would be so silly about me buying my own ring?* Alison asked herself abruptly. *It's not like there's anything sentimental about the matter!*

She noticed the interested tilt of his head and added hastily, ''Sure. Why not? At least that way I know I'll like it. I'm not paying for it, though. There's no room in my budget this month for diamonds. So you'll have to let me know your price range.''

Logan reached into his pocket. ''Maybe it's not necessary. Do you think this will do?'' He tossed a small velvet-covered box at her.

Even though the throw was dead on target, Alison was unprepared, and she almost dropped her coffee in trying to catch the box. She set her cup aside and, with a wary glance at Logan, opened the box.

From the white satin lining, a diamond dinner ring winked up at her. The large center stone was surrounded by a spiral of smaller ones, set in a wide gold band. There was something about the cut of the stones which made her think the ring was old, but the styling of the setting was thoroughly up-to-date.

''This really isn't an engagement ring, you know,'' she said.

Logan shrugged. "So you have unusual tastes. Just like my grandmother."

"It was hers?" *He's right, there's no sense in buying a ring when this one will do,* she told herself. *What's the big deal, Novak?* She took the ring out of the box, slipped it onto her finger, and held her hand up for inspection. The ring felt heavy; it was no wonder, she thought, that jewelers talked of stones!

Then a stray beam of sunshine caught the center diamond and turned its clear brilliance to fire, and she forgot the weight of the ring as she studied its beauty.

"Great." He took another long swallow of coffee. "That just leaves the matter of a wedding date."

Alison stopped turning the ring in the sunshine and looked up. "I hadn't thought—"

"Exactly. Neither of us did, last night. But it would be nice if our stories agreed, don't you think? If you tell people we've decided on next June, and I'm going around saying we're getting married a week from Friday—"

Alison gasped. "A week from... You've got to be joking."

"Actually, yes, I am. I can never predict when I'll be out of the office on Fridays. Saturday would be much better, because that happens to be my weekend off. So unless you have a problem with that—"

She wanted to scream *No!* Instead she took a deep breath and said reasonably, "Don't you think Dr. Sinclair's apt to think it's a bit sudden? Yesterday the whole thing was a secret, today we can't wait to tie the knot—"

"Don't you find it flattering, Alison?" His slow smile lit his face. His eyes glowed and for the first time she noticed a tiny dimple at the corner of his mouth. "You see, it was only when the news burst out of me yesterday that I realized how impatient I've grown during the weeks since we made our engagement official."

"That's a nice twist," Alison admitted.

"Isn't it? So last night I begged you to reconsider your plans for an elaborate ceremony a year from now in favor of a small and intimate one next week. And since you really do want to start a family right away…" His voice softened and deepened. "…And since I can be very persuasive…by the time I was finished, you not only agreed with me, you were as eager to be my wife as I am to claim you for my own."

His voice sounded like warm honey. Which, Alison thought, was probably what the average woman subjected to his particular brand of charm felt like by the time he was finished. She could just imagine the sort of persuasive methods at his command. That soft seductive voice, she was sure, was only the beginning of a long list.

Fortunately for her, Alison had no trouble seeing through the technique.

"You needn't bother," she said. "I'm convinced. A week from Saturday's just fine." Apprehension clenched like a fist in her stomach, but she ruthlessly forced the feeling aside. What difference did it make precisely when they made their agreement legal? Any date he set would have made her feel fluttery.

Last night, when a wedding date had been only an amorphous *someday,* she must have subconsciously concluded that if he found a new practice right away, they might never have to go to such lengths—so it was no wonder she was feeling a bit jittery now that she faced a precise date. In fact, however, she knew that the longer this step was put off, the less likely they were to succeed.

His smile had broadened. "I told you I was persuasive."

Annoyed, Alison struck back. "Not at all. I agreed because the sooner the formalities are out of the way, the sooner you can focus all your attention on looking for a new job—and the sooner we can be done with this."

Logan's eyebrows drew together. "Exactly the reason I'm in such a hurry." He drained his coffee mug. "Want me to put this back in the kitchen?"

"Don't bother. I'll get it." She stood up to see him out. He paused in the doorway and lifted a hand to her cheek as if to turn her face up to his. He was so close that she could see the tiny, faint line which was all that remained of the cut she'd made on his lip. She stared at it, knowing that in another moment his mouth would once again touch hers, just as he had kissed her last night...

Except today there was no reason for it, so what did he think he was doing?

In almost a reflex action, Alison pulled back, and instantly she saw a question come to life in Logan's eyes. One dark eyebrow tilted and he tipped his head to one side as if to study her more closely.

"There isn't an audience today," she pointed out.

"And you thought I was going to kiss you?" He sounded honestly surprised.

Idiot, she told herself. Once again she'd let her imagination run riot. She should have just stood her ground, instead of assuming she knew what he intended.

"Did that kiss last night disturb you so much, then?" Logan didn't wait for an answer. He brushed his fingers down across her cheek.

Alison willed herself to stand absolutely still, but to her dismay she couldn't stop her lip from trembling.

"Amazing," Logan whispered. His fingertip followed the full line of her lower lip, his touch as soft as a butterfly's wing. "Maybe you do have some normal instincts, after all."

Alison knew better than to try to hide in her office. But luck was with her; Kit was out for most of the day, and Susannah was so absorbed in the presentation she was working on that she didn't even come out of the top floor production room for lunch.

It was almost the close of regular business hours when Alison went to the supply closet for a box of paper clips and ran smack into Susannah, who was standing on one of the kitchen chairs while she searched the top shelves.

"You wouldn't happen to know where Rita hid the masking tape, would you?" Susannah asked. "She's gone home already, and I've been digging for a fresh roll for what feels like an hour."

"Here in the middle, where it's easier to reach." Alison pushed a box out of the way so she could get to the tape. She saw the gleam of diamonds on her outstretched hand at the same moment Susannah did, and she bit her lip hard. How had she managed to forget for that one crucial moment the weight of the ring? She shot a look at her partner, but Susannah's face was calm.

"Nice ring. You're getting more pretty new bits of jewelry lately, Ali. First the flute player and now a diamond..." Her eyes widened. "A *diamond* ring. And that's your left hand..."

Alison felt hot blood flooding her face.

The blush was obviously all the confirmation Susannah needed. She leaped down off the chair, turned toward the stairway, and yelled, "Kitty, come quick!"

Kit's head appeared over the banister rail two floors up. "What? Is somebody hurt?"

"Did you know Alison's wearing a diamond ring?" Susannah said breathlessly. "An absolutely gorgeous diamond ring."

Kit looked puzzled. "Are we allowed to know who gave it to her, or do we have to play Twenty Questions?"

"*Twenty?* With all the men Ali knows—and the fact that not a one of them stands out as special—it'd be more like a hundred questions. However, I happen to know who it is.''

The hot blood drained from Alison's face just as quickly as it had flooded over her. How could Susannah be so certain?

Kit clattered down the stairs and peered at the ring. ''Now this line of reasoning I have to hear, Sue.''

''It's simple logic. She was out with Rob Morrow last night, and today she's wearing a new ring, so obviously he popped the question and she said—''

Alison raised her voice. ''It wasn't Rob.''

Susannah frowned. ''No? Then it just happened today? You don't mean one of your *clients*—''

''Of course not.''

Kit was still studying the ring. ''But you *are* engaged, aren't you? You must be, Ali, because I can't see you buying something like this for yourself.''

''Okay, Alison.'' Susannah sounded very patient. ''Let's take this slowly, from the beginning. You went to the opera last night with Rob, right?''

''Well, actually, I forgot all about the opera.''

Kit said, to no one in particular, ''Alison Novak forgot an appointment? Damn, this *is* serious stuff.''

Alison took a deep breath. ''I'm marrying Logan Kavanaugh.''

The silence which filled the brownstone was so intense it was suffocating. Kit sat down so hard on the kitchen chair that it almost tipped over into the supply closet.

Susannah broke the hush finally, with a long sigh. ''Ali, are you quite sure you know him well enough for this? I mean, you're certain he's not…kinky?''

Kit's jaw dropped. ''What in the heck does that mean?''

Susannah said, ''Well, the first thing Ali did was hit him in the mouth so hard she made him bleed. If he's masochistic enough to find that kind of thing attractive—''

Kit rolled her eyes. Alison started to laugh almost uncontrollably. Susannah muttered, "Maybe he's a doctor because he actually *enjoys* the sight of blood."

All of them heard the front door open and close again. "Rita's already gone, isn't she?" Kit asked. "I'll go take care of it."

"No, please," Alison gasped. "Let me. I'll have to pull myself together before I can face a client, and right now that sounds like a very good idea."

"We'll all go," Susannah said. "We're certainly not getting anywhere with this discussion."

"Not when you're being an imbecile," Kit muttered.

Susannah defended herself. "Well, she *doesn't* know him very well."

"Absolutely true. She doesn't know him nearly well enough to marry him. But that doesn't mean he's a—"

Alison cut in. "You're talking about me again as if I'm not here," she said over her shoulder. Then she saw who was waiting near the front door, and she stopped dead on the stairway. "Hello, Logan. I thought you never got off work before eight. And what's that you're holding?"

He was standing in the center of the entrance hall, both arms stiffly extended before him, clutching a glass pie plate in both hands.

He looked down at the plate and said ruefully, "I don't know. A wizened little woman who's about as tall as my elbow was hovering on the porch when I came up. She shoved this at me, muttered something about bringing it in, and fled. It seems to be a little drippy. And it smells like peaches."

"You think everything smells like peaches," Alison said. In this case, however, he was right; when she rescued the glass plate from his grasp and looked down at a perfectly browned pie, a wave of aroma caught her. She could smell not only peaches but cinnamon and nutmeg.

Susannah said, "Now *that's* interesting. I thought Ali was the one with the fetish for peaches."

"It had to be Mrs. Holcomb," Alison said. "I gave her the fruit, and she baked a pie and actually brought it over."

Logan was looking very confused.

Alison took pity on him. "We've seen her set foot off her own property just once before, and she only did that because she thought she'd nabbed a criminal. It's incredible that she'd come out of her house simply to deliver a pie."

Kit murmured, "Good heavens, I suppose next she'll be buying a ticket for Paris."

"Both of you are ignoring the real subject," Susannah announced. She braced herself against the newel post. "Dr. Kavanaugh, exactly why do you want to marry Alison?"

Alison gave him credit; he didn't flinch. "I believe I've already answered that question to my fiancée's satisfaction," he pointed out.

"So, in other words, Sue," Kit murmured, "mind your own business. It *is* going to be a long engagement, right, Logan?"

"Terribly long," Logan said. "At least it is from my point of view. Darling, I'm still a bit sticky from that pie, and if you don't set it down soon you'll probably be permanently glued to the glass. Can I take it somewhere?"

"Exactly *how* long?" Susannah asked suspiciously.

Logan considered. "Well, I'd have to look at a calendar to count it up—but I think it's nine whole days. Is that right, my dear?" *Here's your cue,* his direct look seemed to be saying.

A good deal of the success of the plan, Alison reminded herself, depended on the next few minutes, and whether she could make her partners believe that this was a real—if hurried—engagement. If she couldn't convince Susannah and Kit, it was probable that others—people like Burt

Sinclair—would be just as suspicious. But if she could get Sue and Kitty firmly on her side…

Alison forced herself to smile. "Eight, if you don't count the actual wedding day," she said. "I don't like to add it in, myself—that extra twenty-four hours makes it sound so much farther away."

Logan looked as if he'd like to applaud.

Kit put both hands to her head. "Alison. Alison, you can't do this."

"And just think, Kitty," Susannah groaned, "we've always said Ali was the *practical* one!"

CHAPTER SIX

IN THE sudden silence which descended on Tryad, Alison turned on her heel and carried the peach pie downstairs to the kitchen. Logan was right behind her.

He went straight to the sink to scrub the sticky peach juice from his hands. "Well, that's done," he said.

"Done? Breaking the news to Kit and Susannah, you mean?" Alison shook her head. "Oh, no. They've only started." She put her hands under the stream of hot water.

"What did Susannah mean when she said you're the practical one?"

"Oh, it's just a joke about the way our strengths balance each other out. That's why it's such a great partnership. We all take care of our own clients, but we work well as a team, too. Susannah's the visionary who can pull out one creative notion after another. Kit's the technician who can translate Sue's ideas into solid form and sell them to a client. And I'm the one who watches the budget and collects slow-pay accounts, and makes sure even when we're working on a tight deadline that everyone eats and sleeps. Stuff like that."

"The practical one." He sounded very thoughtful. "I'm glad to know it."

He was laughing inside; Alison knew, because she could see the glint of humor in his eyes. But she couldn't detect even a trace of irony in his voice.

Well, if that amused him, she could play along. "Sometimes we put it a little differently—Susannah's the sense of humor, Kit's the tender heart, I'm the calculating brain." She found a roll of plastic wrap and swathed the pie tightly to keep it fresh. "And you think I'm being a lot more calculating than practical about the baby, don't you?"

"You're granting me the right to an opinion? I thought you'd put an end to that discussion some time ago."

"I did. But I'm sure a little detail like that wouldn't change your views in the slightest. In any case, just to keep things clear—we made a deal, and I don't intend to let you go back on it. Now, what are you doing here? If you're going to start dropping in on me every fifteen minutes—"

"Don't exaggerate. Twice in a whole day is hardly—" He paused and added thoughtfully, "Though the fact that you feel I'm ever-present does have certain interesting implications."

Alison cut in before he could pursue the idea. "Not flattering ones, I assure you. So what did you forget this time?"

"Sure you want to discuss it right here?"

She glanced over her shoulder. "You're right. Susannah has the most sensitive ears I've ever encountered outside a bat colony. Let me clear my desk and we can go have coffee."

She paused in the hallway to neaten the supply closet enough to close the door, and went on into her office to put her files away. Logan followed her. He stood just inside the door for a moment, and then he nodded and crossed the room to sit down on the wicker love seat.

"What's that nod mean?" The question was out before Alison could stop herself. "Approval, or confirmation?" *And what do I care?* she asked herself.

"It's just about what I expected."

Which was no answer at all, Alison thought. With no regard for order, she swept up the project she'd been working on and dropped the folder into a drawer. "I'm ready. Where are we going?"

"How about right here?"

"I thought you were worried about privacy."

"The kitchen did seem to echo. But a coffee shop isn't going to be a lot better. Here, on the other hand..." He patted the cushion beside him. "Come and sit down. I've been thinking..."

Reluctantly, she joined him on the love seat, settling on the edge of the cushion. "You know it sends shivers up my spine when you say you've been thinking. What's on your mind this time?"

"For one thing, am I supposed to rent a fancy tux? Because if so, I'd better get an order in while there's still time for alterations."

"*That's* so personal and private you couldn't ask over a cup of coffee? No, you don't need a tuxedo. This is not going to be a party. Nobody's going to be there...." She paused and added, "Are they?"

"We don't want it to look like a hole and corner sort of affair, do we?"

"It wouldn't bother me any." She caught the sound of footsteps coming down the stairs, and shot Logan a warning look. "I'll bet it's Susannah," she whispered.

"Coming to spy?" He slid an arm around her waist and pulled her to him, till her back was pressed against his chest. Her heartbeat was skittering all over the place; his was strong and steady. Alison knew because she was pressed so tightly against him that she could feel the steady rhythm pulsing against her spine.

He bent his head, leaning his cheek against her hair. "If the wedding's too private it'll look distinctly fishy," he warned softly.

"What's your definition of *too private?*"

He didn't answer. "I also wanted to apologize for setting the date without even thinking about your family or considering whether it will be a hardship on them to come on such short notice. If it is—"

Alison's voice was curt and crisp. "Don't worry about my family. Just how elaborate an affair do you have in mind?"

"How much will it take to be convincing?"

"To Burt Sinclair? Not a lot, I should think."

"How about my parents?"

Alison pulled away. "You're not serious. You're going to try to delude your *parents* into thinking this is real?"

"We agreed we weren't going to tell anybody it wasn't."

"Your mother isn't just anybody, Logan."

"All right. *You* can explain our little deal to her." He drew her to him again, tucking her against his side this time with one arm draped casually over her shoulders.

"Oh, no."

"I'd like to listen in, of course. I particularly want to see her face when you get to the part about the baby."

"You've made your point, Kavanaugh. Of course, you realize you're going to have to explain it sometime—right?"

"Oh, yes. But once it's all over I can throw myself on her sympathy about how deceived I was, how foolish, not to see you as the heartless and calculating woman you are."

Alison tensed like bent steel.

"Stings, does it?" Logan said. "Truth often does."

"I can certainly see why you'd rather wait and present yourself as the victim instead of admitting that you're equally heartless and calculating."

"Of course I would," Logan said easily. "It *is* my mother we're talking about, and I'd like her to continue to cherish certain illusions about me. The additional advantage of playing it this way is—if we're lucky—she'll never even know about the baby."

Alison blinked. "Whether she knows or not, obviously it's going to be none of her business."

"Ah, but she might not see it that way. I'm an only child,

and my mother is a frustrated grandmother-in-waiting. So if there's the merest hint that there is an infant who might be in any way connected with me—''

''I'll sign a confession, all right?'' Alison said dryly.

''I'm glad you understand. Let's just hope it isn't necessary to go quite that far. Now where the guest list is concerned, there are about two dozen people I'll have to invite. If you have the same—''

''I was thinking more in terms of two participants, two witnesses, and a judge.'' She sighed. ''All right. I'll see what I can do to even up the numbers. And I suppose you want a reception of some sort? Will champagne and cake be good enough, or do we need a sit-down, six-course dinner?''

''Alison, darling—it doesn't have to be the production of the century. I'll help, of course.''

''When are you going to fit it in?'' Alison said wryly. ''In any case, I think you've already been quite helpful enough.''

''I've tried. For one thing, I've done my best to clear your calendar—I convinced Burt he doesn't need a PR firm after all.''

''Oh, that's just great. You've arranged for me to trade a paying job for one that's going to cost a bundle.''

''I'll take care of the bills. And anyway, just think of the difficulty of advising Burt, under the circumstances....'' He rubbed his chin gently against her hair, and then laid his cheek against the soft glossiness.

Alison pulled away and looked up at him with eyes narrowed.

''I thought I heard footsteps again,'' he murmured.

''Well, I didn't.''

''Really?'' He tucked her head under his cheek once more and said with a yawn, ''Your hair feels just like black satin.''

"Don't get too comfortable."

"On this love seat? You've got to be kidding." He released her and stood up to stretch.

Alison thought he looked impossibly tall, standing there above her with arms extended and muscles tensed. She could see the bulge of biceps even under the long sleeves of his pin-striped shirt.

"It's a good thing this isn't going to last," he mused. "I'd have to buy you a couch so I'd be comfortable when I come to visit."

"Go ahead and be a sport," Alison said tartly. "Make it a daybed."

His long, slow smile gave way to a yawn.

He *did* look tired, Alison thought. "Go home and get some sleep," she ordered, and wondered why she sounded just a little gruff.

"Can't," he said through another yawn. "Not for a while, at least. I've got four new mothers to check on. I'll talk to you tomorrow, all right?"

"Why does the very thought make me feel shaky?"

Logan's brows drew together, but the gleam in his eyes negated the frown. "I don't know, but we could do some experiments to see if we can isolate the stimulus—"

"Not that kind of shaky. I'm just trying to anticipate what tomorrow's *surprise de jour* will be. The Mormon Tabernacle Choir?"

"What a glorious idea! Will you call them, or shall I?"

Alison flung a pillow at him. Logan ducked, grinned, and departed.

As they helped Alison dress for her wedding, Kit was unusually silent and Susannah even more of a chatterbox than normal. Alison knew it was only a matter of time before one or the other of them gave up her self-imposed restraint in favor of plain speaking; she was amazed they'd been able to control themselves this long.

As she sat at the dressing table in her bedroom, carefully outlining her mouth with a new shade of lip color, Alison tried to guess which of them would crack first. Susannah's frown was tiny, but it cut deep lines into her forehead. Kit's jaw was clenched so tight her teeth must ache.

Alison felt horrible about deceiving them. Their partnership had been built on trust and caring, but now she was breaking faith with her best friends by letting them think she was going into this marriage starry-eyed and swept off her feet…and probably doomed to early disappointment.

Of course, she reminded herself, telling them the truth wouldn't be all that much better. In fact, she could think of only one difference: as soon as Kit and Susannah realized they need no longer tiptoe around Alison's supposed feelings for her husband-to-be, all restraint would be gone. They'd be every bit as horrified about the deal she and Logan had really made as they were about the supposedly romantic sudden wedding, and they wouldn't hesitate to say so.

No, things were better left as they were. Alison could never explain; only time would convince her friends that she did indeed know what she was doing, and that her choice was the right one. In a year or so, when Logan was gone from her life and she had her baby instead—and was obviously happy to have it so—they would begin to understand.

She looked once more at Susannah's frown and Kit's clenched jaw, and a rush of thankfulness swept over her. She was fortunate indeed to have these two people. She hated to cause pain to friends who loved her so much that they fretted about her happiness and worried that she was being a fool and bit their tongues to keep from arguing with her.

"It's going to be fine, you know," Alison said.

"That does it." Susannah set a hairbrush down on the dressing table with unnecessary force. "I absolutely cannot stand here any longer and pretend that I'm happy about this. For heaven's sake, Ali, I thought you had good sense."

"You think it's awful that we're not going to have a honeymoon," Alison said.

Susannah shook her head. "Not at all. And I'm not even objecting because he's moving into your house. I think it's crazy, but—"

"I own the row house. He's been renting an apartment. What's so crazy about using my place and subletting his?"

"I said it's not the house that bothers me. It's the whole idea of getting married so suddenly. Do you know Rita was so surprised when she heard the news that she dropped a stack of five hundred letters? It took the two of us half an hour just to pick them up, and then she said…" Sue's voice trailed off.

The pause was intriguing. "You can't stop there, Sue. What did she say?"

"Something about you being in the biggest hurry of us all to get married, as if you'd waited till last so you could hold the record for all time."

"Sue," Kit said.

"Why can't you wait awhile, Ali? Make sure this is real, that it's not just stardust in your eyes—"

Alison reached for her eye shadow. "Sue, did I get in your way when you wanted to marry Marc?"

"I'd known Marc for the best part of a decade! You've known Logan Kavanaugh for—gee, I'd guess it's been at least twenty minutes. For heaven's sake, you only met his parents last night."

"I'm not marrying his parents, Sue. And since they only arrived yesterday, I could hardly meet them earlier."

Kit intervened. "Sue, if you'll hand me Ali's jacket—"

Susannah wasn't to be sidetracked. "How did he propose, anyway?"

Straight out of a logic textbook, Alison wanted to say. She finished tipping her lashes with a second coat of mascara and put the tube away. "Nicely—over dinner at Cicero's. And if you expect me to share the details, forget it."

Susannah sighed. "You know, I'd have been happier if you'd actually advertised for a husband as I always thought you would."

"Advertised? You mean in the Personals?"

"No, I was thinking more in terms of *Help Wanted.*"

That, Alison thought, cut rather uncomfortably close to the truth. She touched a powder brush to her nose and stood up.

"At least that way," Susannah went on, "you wouldn't be caught up in this incredible enchantment, so you wouldn't expect it to last, and you wouldn't be disappointed when it inevitably doesn't."

I've been convincing, Alison told herself, *if Sue is so positive I'm enchanted with Logan...*

Kit held up the jacket of Alison's ice-pink raw silk suit for her to slip into. "Sue, the box with Ali's flowers is down in the living room. Would you go and get it, please?"

Susannah muttered something under her breath and headed for the stairs.

Alison patted her lapels into place and adjusted the scoop neckline of the raspberry camisole. "I wonder if Mrs. Holcomb will be at the chapel. I invited her, you know, when I took her pie plate back. She seemed pleased to be asked, and since she's starting to come out of her shell—"

"Stop changing the subject, Ali." Kit's voice was firm. "You know very well Sue's right. You hardly know him."

"I know enough."

"You investigate your clients more thoroughly than this!"

"I thought he was your friend, Kitty."

"Yes, he is, and so are you. You're both wonderful people, and I want to see you both happy. So call this off, Ali."

"Can't," Alison said crisply.

"Of course you can. Sue and I will back you up. It might be embarrassing for a little while, but in the long run..."

"I know what I'm doing, Kitty."

"I'm sure you think so, but..." Kit sighed. "Darling, I don't know how to say this without sounding condescending and patronizing, but if you're getting married just because Sue and I did and you're suddenly feeling left out... Please don't."

That was almost funny, Alison thought. Envy of her partners' solid, loving marriages was one of the few bad reasons which *hadn't* influenced her decision.

Kit said gently, "You just need to have a little faith that the right man will come along."

The right man? That's exactly what I don't want, Alison thought. "Logan is precisely what I've been looking for."

"I know you're convinced now, but.... Ali, I don't want you to regret this."

"Believe me—I won't." Alison reached out to take both of Kit's hands. "Please, just be happy for me, Kitty."

Kit sighed. "You're going to go through with this despite it all, aren't you? All right, I've done my best and I'll shut up now. The last thing I want to do is undermine what little chance of success this marriage has by nagging at you about it. I promise I won't even say *I told you so* when it falls apart."

Susannah spoke from the doorway. "I, on the other hand, have made no such vow." She held out a small white box.

"One nosegay, trailing raspberry ribbon—at least he got that right. And the limousine's here."

The car whisked them the few blocks to a tiny chapel which was becoming something of a tradition at Tryad. Kit and Susannah had both been married here, as well, and Alison knew that all three of them were remembering, and comparing—not the size of the flower arrangements or the style of the bride's dress, but the emotion which sizzled in the air.

Logan was waiting for her at the door, so they could walk up the aisle together. When she'd asked him to do that, she'd thought for a moment that he was going to cross-examine her about why there wasn't a father or brother or uncle to do the honors.

But he hadn't; he'd simply agreed—and she'd felt such a surge of gratitude that she'd almost thrown her arms around him. That same thankfulness swept over her now. Not, of course, that she was actually about to embrace him…

He looked wonderful in a dark gray suit, sporting a tie and pocket handkerchief the precise shade of her raspberry camisole. She hadn't expected that tiny note of unity, and a trickle of warmth seeped through her.

Logan tucked her hand into the bend of his arm and said very softly, "Are you okay?"

His eyes were dark, earnest. Alison felt a bit somber herself, but—conscious of their audience—she smiled up at him. "I'd rather be at the football game."

Gold flecks lit the emerald of his eyes, and humor tugged at every line of his face. "*That's* what I forgot. The Bears are in town, too. We could have made the game if we'd only planned the party for this morning."

That way it would be over by now, Alison thought. *And my stomach wouldn't feel as if it's hosting a moderate earthquake.*

The organist began to play. Alison's hands were shaking; she was grateful to have Logan and the little nosegay to cling to. Suddenly the chapel felt like Yankee Stadium on the first day of the World Series. Most of the crowd was a blur, but here and there Alison saw individual faces. Rob Morrow was sitting in an aisle seat with his arms folded across his chest, staring straight ahead. Jake, the pal who always had a funny story, was toward the back, almost in a corner. Kit was trying very hard to smile. Susannah wasn't even making an attempt to look anything other than skeptical. At the very front of the chapel, Logan's parents were watching intently. His mother was clutching a lacy handkerchief as if she fully expected to need it.

The first few minutes of the ceremony were a blur to Alison, but suddenly the fog seemed to clear and she found herself looking up at Logan, holding his hand, and making promises she had no intention of keeping.

Her knees trembled at the audacity of what they were doing. Then she reminded herself that at its heart marriage was nothing more than a legal contract. And wasn't it a truism of the law that no contract could be made to last forever? Surely she'd read somewhere that every agreement was required to have an ending point, no matter how far off. All she and Logan had done was make an agreement which would end a little earlier than most.

Her voice was strong as she finished her vows, and that current of certainty carried her well into the formalities of greeting their guests on the steps of the chapel after the ceremony was over. She even smiled with complete sincerity at Burt Sinclair as he introduced his wife, a tall woman with upswept blond hair and cold blue eyes.

"Do you play bridge, Alison?" Mrs. Sinclair asked crisply.

"Not very well, I'm afraid."

"The wives of all the doctors in the practice get together

twice a week for a few hands.'' Mrs. Sinclair's voice was as chilly as her eyes. ''But perhaps it's for the best that you don't play, since you're the fifth and an uneven table is so difficult to manage. Still, it would be nice to have a substitute.'' She moved on before Alison could do more than blink in surprise.

Burt Sinclair lingered a moment longer. ''You two got in a bit of a rush with this wedding, didn't you?''

Logan stepped closer, sliding one arm around Alison's shoulders and with the other hand raising her fingers to his lips to kiss the wedding ring he'd slid into place beside the diamond cluster. ''Didn't I tell you we're anxious to start a family?''

Alison looked up at him, intending to add her approval with a smile. His eyes were alight with a glow which said— to the average observer, at least—that he couldn't wait to get her home and take her to bed. Even though Alison had expected he'd concoct something of the kind, she was almost mesmerized by his gaze.

She hardly heard Burt Sinclair announce that he wouldn't be surprised—what with the speed of the wedding—if some people thought they'd already begun the family in question. And she barely noticed when he moved on toward the sidewalk where his wife stood tapping her shoe against the concrete. Not until that high-voltage gaze of Logan's settled back to normal could she draw a full breath, and even then she couldn't stop looking at him.

''How long have you worked with Dr. Sinclair?'' she asked finally.

''Three years, give or take.''

''And presumably you've known his wife about that long, too?''

''I suppose so. Why?''

''And it didn't dawn on you till last week that he's crude and she's cold and manipulative? Where've you been,

Kavanaugh, that you didn't happen to notice a little thing like that?''

Logan shrugged. ''It never mattered before.''

Alison wanted to groan.

She'd thought all the guests had gone, but suddenly Logan said, under his breath, ''Trouble off the port side,'' and she glanced to her left to see his mother only steps away.

Alison didn't quite see why he was anticipating a problem; it had been plain last night that Logan adored his mother. Then she realized that Camilla Kavanaugh's gaze was at the moment just as farseeing as Logan at his sharpest, and his comment made sense. No wonder he expected trouble. If Camilla Kavanaugh been within hearing range when Burt Sinclair had made his less-than-tactful statement implying that Alison was already expecting a child, what would the woman Logan had described as a frustrated grandmother-in-waiting have to say about it?

Alison braced herself.

''I thought you and Dad had gone on to the reception,'' Logan said. ''Or do you want a limousine ride?''

''Oh, no—I wouldn't dream of playing chaperon. I just thought perhaps someone should stick around to make sure you two remembered where you were supposed to go next.'' Camilla smiled mischievously and strolled off to where Logan's father waited.

In the limousine, Alison sank wearily into the soft black leather seat. ''I'd never have thought of just not appearing for the reception,'' she said. ''Do you suppose we could have gotten by with it, and gone straight home instead?''

Home. The word seemed to echo in the limousine, and in Alison's mind. It held an entirely different meaning now.

Tonight, she would not be going home alone. And not only tonight, but for the foreseeable future.

She looked from the corner of her eye at the man who

was now her husband, and a tinge of panic flickered through her veins.

By the time the reception was over and the limousine delivered them to the row house, Alison's panic had given way to pure exhaustion. The only emotion she was capable of feeling was guilt; there was no shortage of that, because Logan's mother had hugged her as they said goodbye and called her *my precious new daughter*...

The moment the door opened, the gray Persian came bounding down the stairs, noisily demanding her dinner. Alison scooped up the cat and began to stroke the soft fur. Her fingers were still trembling a bit; Ashes seemed fascinated and stretched out her soft paw to stroke Alison's hand. On the top step, the black cat sat upright, his tail curved elegantly around his body, watching.

Logan closed the door and held out the key on his open palm. Alison shook her head. "That one's yours."

His hand closed so slowly over the key that Alison wondered if he saw it not as a simple way to open a door but as a symbol of more—of, perhaps, other kinds of doors.

She raised her gaze to meet his, and suddenly the foyer seemed small and closed-in and stuffy, as if there wasn't room for both of them. Her heart was pounding, and she felt almost faint. If he reached out for her...

She hurried into the living room, the cat still in her arms, and stood in the center of the enormous space, trying not to gulp for air, trying to pretend that everything was normal.

She looked down at the black cat, winding his body sinuously around her ankles. There was a tiny tremor in her voice as she said, "Are you hungry, too, Velvet?"

"You look absolutely exhausted," Logan said. "Tell me where to find their food, and I'll take care of it."

She told him. His fingers brushed her wrist as he lifted

Ashes out of her arms; Alison felt as if she'd been scorched, but Logan showed no reaction at all.

For a long moment after he'd gone, Alison stood in the center of the room and stared at nothing. The sizzling looks, the possessive touches...he'd been performing for an audience, that was all. Now there was no audience, and she had nothing to fear. She'd been a fool to have so much as a qualm about it.

As if he'd want to complicate his life that way, she told herself. *You're perfectly safe, and you should appreciate knowing it.*

She kicked off her shoes and sank into the nearest chair, rubbing her temples. The grandfather clock in the corner struck seven, and she looked up, startled. Could that possibly be the right time? It felt much later.

And how were they to get through the rest of the evening, this first and most difficult?

She sighed and stood up again to follow him. In the kitchen, Logan was leaning against the breakfast bar, his back to the living room, watching the cats gobble their dinner.

He's just as uncomfortable as I am, she thought, and immediately she felt a little better. "If you're hungry—"

"After all those hors d'oeuvres at the reception?" He smiled faintly. "Or do you mean you are? You can't have eaten much, that's sure. I'm sorry I didn't think to get dinner reservations."

"It's not important. There's food here."

"There's always Cicero's."

He doesn't want to spend the evening here, Alison thought. *And I can certainly sympathize.*

"Or we could try Coq Au Vin," Logan went on. "You seemed to be a favorite with the new owner, so maybe he'd find us a table."

"I'm only a favorite because of the singles club. He

knows that every other Saturday night the Chicago Singles will add an obscene amount to his—'' She stopped abruptly.

"Alison? What's the matter?"

She put both hands to her head, where a nagging little twinge was rapidly growing into a major migraine. "Please tell me it hasn't been two weeks since that ridiculous first meeting.''

"I suppose I can tell you, but it has. Do you mean—" Logan started to laugh. "You're supposed to be at a Singles meeting *tonight?*"

"Don't let it bother you," Alison said over her shoulder. She stepped into her shoes, wincing at the way the leather pinched in all the wrong places. "There's no need for you to go. In any case, you're not eligible anymore.''

"Then neither are you," Logan pointed out.

"That's different. I'm in charge of the darn thing, at least till it gets a bit more established. I have to be there.''

"Well, I'm absolutely not allowing my bride to go out alone on our wedding night. What kind of man do you think I am?''

Alison looked out the front door. The wind had risen, and a few leaves, fallen before their time, scattered across the sidewalk. She reached into the closet for a raincoat. "What do you mean, *allow?* And it's not as if I need protection, you know.''

"You're right," Logan admitted. "I'm hardly in any position to argue about what you do, and you probably don't need a bodyguard. Nevertheless, I'm going—mostly because I'm dying to hear how you explain to all those lonely single people exactly why you're so late to their party.''

CHAPTER SEVEN

SUNLIGHT streaming in her window woke Alison, and she rolled over to let the rays warm her face. For a moment she basked in the golden glow, and then she remembered. She sat up straight, listening intently for sounds from downstairs—but all was silent.

That wasn't surprising. The view from the guest room, just below her bedroom, was nearly the same as hers, but the draperies were heavy enough to shut out the light completely. If Logan had closed them last night, and if he was as tired as she suspected, he might sleep for hours yet.

And if she had any sense, Alison told herself, she'd pull the blankets over her head and go back to sleep, too. Instead, she piled the pillows against the white velvet headboard of her bed and reached for a book from her bedside table.

But she didn't open it. She leaned back into the pillows instead and—without success—tried not to relive the events of the evening before.

The Singles meeting had been an unmitigated disaster. Not only had she arrived a full hour late—after a number of the singles had already left—but she'd been completely unprepared. And though during her years at Tryad she'd learned to think on her feet, she'd been too tired and overwrought last night to respond effectively to a couple of members who'd wanted to make a federal case out of her mistake.

She thought it over and shrugged. Either the members would forgive her lapse and come back in two weeks for

the next regular meeting, or they wouldn't. In either case, there wasn't much she could do about it now.

After the fiasco of the Singles club, she'd thought nothing could get worse. But the crowning touch had been yet to come.

By the time they got back to the row house, Alison had been walking around in a daze so complete that she'd simply pointed to the guest room and said, "If you don't want company, make sure the door is closed tight." She'd been upstairs in her own room before it dawned on her that Logan might not realize she'd been talking about the cats.

She'd been too tired even to blush, much less go back down and try to explain. This morning was a little different; she could feel the warmth rising in her face.

Well, she'd just have to get over it, that was all. That incident had been mild, really—and there were apt to be a lot more of them. Any time two people lived in close proximity there were going to be misunderstandings, comments that could be taken more than one way. No one could watch every single word, not over any period of time. And considering the special circumstances under which she and Logan were living...

"There are no special circumstances," she corrected herself. There must be thousands of coed roommates in the city, men and women who shared living space without also sharing a closer relationship. She and Logan were no different than the rest. All the meaningless words they'd said yesterday didn't change the facts—any more than the kiss they had shared at the end of the ceremony had promised intimacies yet to come.

Even though that kiss had been far from the innocuous brush of the lips that she'd expected. That was easily explained, after all; when he'd embraced her as if he was dying of thirst and she was the oasis that would save him,

Logan had just been making sure that their audience had no reason to ask uncomfortable questions.

No, the events of yesterday made no difference whatsoever. She'd just keep reminding herself that they were roommates, nothing more nor less. If she were sharing her house with anyone other than Logan, she'd get up this morning, make coffee, take some cinnamon rolls out of the freezer, get the newspaper from the front step...

She slumped against the pile of pillows and thought about doing those things. But she didn't move.

It's too early, she told herself. *And I didn't sleep very well.*

That was certainly true. Despite her exhaustion she'd had trouble dozing off; she kept thinking she heard Logan moving around, which pulled her back to full wakefulness.

When she had finally slept, she'd had the dream again. Only this time, the crowd of guests at the birthday party had been so dense that she couldn't even get close enough to see the child. All she could do was stand there holding the cake and watching as the three small candles which decorated it burned down till they were nothing but dark wax puddles against the white icing.

She'd roused to find her face wet with tears—and even now she had an almost overwhelming urge to bury her face in the pillows and sob. Which was very odd, considering that she was now so much closer to her goal.

Or was she?

The question echoed strangely through her mind, and Alison frowned and tried to reason herself out of her blue funk. True, the wedding had been only a small first step toward achieving both her goal and Logan's, but it was an important one...

A small first step—but it was also a massive hurdle. Now she realized what had been tugging at her subconscious all along. She *wasn't* closer to her goal right now than she had been before; in fact, she was even farther away.

So long as she was married, any child of hers would be—in the eyes of the law—Logan's, as well. His legal rights would be automatic. And even if he was willing to give up those rights at the moment, nothing said he couldn't change his mind and pursue them later. Alison was squarely back where she'd started.

No, she realized. She was even worse off, with an extra problem to deal with—for now there was Logan's mother to be considered. What was it he'd said? *She's a frustrated grandmother-in-waiting... If there's the merest hint that there is an infant who might be in any way connected with me...*

Now that Alison had met Camilla Kavanaugh, she had no doubt that Logan was right. Camilla had wholeheartedly embraced a new daughter-in-law she'd known for less than a full day. A woman who was capable of that wouldn't even wait till Alison's child was born before staking her claim as grandma; she'd fall in love the moment she knew about the baby.

And she wasn't likely to let go of her attachment even if her son refused to claim his supposed rights. She might break her heart over it, but she wouldn't give up.

Alison couldn't do that to Camilla Kavanaugh. Not after the way she'd taken Alison to her heart without even knowing her, accepting her on simple faith because she was supposedly so special to Logan. The breakup of the marriage would hurt her badly enough. Now that she'd actually met Camilla, Alison thought Logan was incredibly shortsighted not to have recognized the effect the whole thing would have on his mother. And though she couldn't do anything about that, she could resolve not to add anything more to Camilla Kavanaugh's pain.

She would have to wait until the marriage was over, that

was all. It wasn't the end of the world; Logan's search might take no time at all, and the moment the divorce was complete…

She was so wrapped up in her planning that she almost didn't hear the soft tap on her door. She didn't answer; she sat bolt upright and watched in fascinated disbelief as the knob slowly turned and the door opened a few inches.

Logan said, "Good, you're already awake. I didn't want to knock too loudly and disturb you, but I know you like your coffee fresh, so I brought a cup."

Alison was too stunned even to answer. He came quietly across the room to hand her a steaming mug. He was more casually dressed than she'd ever seen him, wearing faded jeans and a pullover shirt only a couple of shades lighter than his eyes, and neither shoes nor socks. Ashes followed him in and leaped up onto the bed to nuzzle at Alison's hand.

Alison cradled the mug and sniffed the coffee's fresh aroma. "Thanks. I'm not used to this kind of treatment." *Stupid*, she told herself. *You couldn't have come up with anything dumber to say if you'd had a year to think it over.*

"Well, it's nice to be the first." A smile tugged at the corner of his mouth. "Mind if I sit down and talk a minute?"

She knew it wasn't a good idea, but she couldn't think of any logical reason to refuse. If he'd been planning a seduction attempt, she told herself tartly, he probably wouldn't have waited till this morning. And he obviously would have known better than to present her with a weapon—in the form of boiling hot coffee—before he made his move.

"Go ahead," she said.

He didn't sit, exactly; Alison would have called it *lounging* instead. He looked incredibly at ease as he sprawled across the width of the bed and propped himself on one elbow, close enough that she had no trouble seeing the tiny white scar on his lip. His hand moved sensually across the Persian's long fur; Ashes tilted her head and looked immensely pleased when he started to scratch her chin.

Alison pulled the blankets a little higher and drew her knees up to her chest. ''I hope this isn't your usual bedside manner.''

For a moment she thought he was too busy surveying every visible inch of her even to answer. ''It certainly isn't the usual sort of bed. Where do you buy sheets for this thing? At the tent store?''

''It's the largest bed which would fit in the room.'' She told herself it was silly to feel defensive. ''I like to have plenty of space around me, that's all.''

''I can see that.'' He sounded thoughtful. ''And it obviously applies in your choice of pajamas, too.''

Never had Alison been so grateful that her taste ran to oversize, masculine-tailored nightshirts instead of frilly negligees. If Logan was disappointed, that was just too bad.

She said abruptly, ''I hope you slept well.''

''Not particularly. I kept waiting for the company you promised.''

Alison could feel the hot blood surging up her throat and into her cheeks, but she did her best to ignore it and keep her voice level. ''They're probably just not quite used to you yet, but watch out when they get comfortable. Ashes makes a habit of leaning against any closed door she runs across, just in case the latch isn't quite in place. Velvet, on the other hand, actually turns the doorknob—I've watched him do it.'' *Stop babbling,* she told herself. *You're talking too fast and too much.*

''Oh,'' Logan said. ''You meant the cats?''

He was laughing at her; the sparks in his eyes were a dead giveaway.

Alison pulled her knees even higher and wrapped her

arms around them. "I assume there was something specific you wanted to talk about?"

"Well, yes. I was thinking about this deal of ours, and—"

"I don't believe I like the sound of this," Alison muttered. "If you're telling me, now that I've done my share, that you don't want to keep your part of the bargain—"

"It isn't that—a promise is a promise. But there's some difficulty with the medical route you want to take. It's just occurred to me that I can't exactly have you come to the office as a regular patient."

Alison frowned. "You mean now that we're technically married you can't ethically treat me?"

"Actually, I could. There's a big difference between a doctor who treats his wife and one who sees a patient socially. It's still not a very good idea, but—"

"So what's the problem?"

"It's not ethics that has me stumped, it's practicality. Would you really want your records on file in the chart room?"

Alison drew a deep breath. "I presume you mean Dr. Sinclair could see the whole thing?"

"All of the doctors have access, in case they need to see someone else's patient in an emergency."

Alison thought it over as she sipped her coffee. "You're not really worried about my sensitive feelings, though, are you, Logan? You're afraid your cover will be blown."

He didn't even blink before admitting it. "In a word, yes. And I don't see any way around it. I suppose I could lose your chart for a while, but that can't go on for long. And I can't falsify the records, because that would mean putting my license at risk."

"So what you're telling me is that I'll have to wait." Alison reminded herself that the disappointment which stabbed at her made no sense whatsoever; she'd come to precisely the same conclusion, hadn't she?

"I don't see any way around it. I'm sorry, Alison. I swear just as soon as it's possible—"

She took pity on him, but not enough to share the fact that she'd reasoned her way to the same result. Having Logan feeling just a bit in her debt might come in handy later on. "I'll hold you to that."

The concern which had shadowed Logan's eyes diminished. "You're not furious?"

"What good would that do?" Her coffee had cooled; she took a sip and wrinkled her nose. "Now, if I'm not going to stay in bed all day…"

Logan grinned. "Don't let me stop you from getting up." But with the lithe, easy movement of one of her cats, he pushed himself up from the bed.

Alison watched him leave the room. He looked just as good in the faded old jeans as he had in the scrubs he'd been wearing in the emergency room the night they'd met—which was to say, even better than he did in ordinary clothes.

She frowned. It seemed a bit odd, but she hadn't realized till now that she'd even noticed—through the immensity of her pain—that the back view of her new doctor was every bit as attractive as the front.…

Alison pushed the blankets back and walked across the room to her closet, flipping through the row of hangers and searching for something she wanted to wear.

In a way, she thought, it was too bad that she'd had to deliberately eliminate every man she knew from the ranks of possible fathers for her baby. Take Logan, for instance; his was just the sort of biological heritage she'd like for her child. His intelligence, his looks, even his slightly twisted sense of humor…

A silky blouse slid through her suddenly numb fingers

to make a sensual puddle at her feet, and Alison started to laugh.

Someday, she thought, when this was all over, she'd really have to share that joke with Logan. He'd probably find it just as hysterically funny as she did.

Alison tried on three different blouses, toyed with her hair, and put on more makeup than she'd worn on a Sunday in as long as she could remember—all the while knowing that the longer she put off going downstairs the more difficult it would be.

Think roommate, she ordered herself as she started down the stairs. *That's all you have to remember.*

Logan was sitting in an overstuffed chair near the bottom of the stairs, with the Sunday newspaper spread around him as if a whirlwind had caught it. She'd reached only the third step down when he lowered the sports section a trifle and looked over the top of the page at her.

Alison hadn't realized, when she'd arranged her living room, what a perfect view of the stairway one could get from that chair by merely turning one's head. But then she'd never had occasion to sit there and watch someone descend.

In fact, she couldn't remember ever having anyone waiting there and watching for her; she had to be downstairs already, in order to let her guests in.

Her knees felt just a little weak, as if she were a model making her first-ever trip down the runway, with a thousand eyes on her. Though, she thought wryly, if she had her choice, she'd opt for a thousand eyes instead of the single pair she had to deal with. It didn't help that Logan wasn't smiling. He looked very serious indeed as he watched.

Alison hoped he realized that she'd only bothered with her hair and her makeup in order to waste a little time.

Heaven help them both if Logan got the idea she was trying to impress him!

It was too bad, she thought, that he *wasn't* on duty this weekend. She'd like to order up a set of triplets—or something equally time-consuming—just to give herself a chance to take a long, quiet breath without being observed.

Fortunately, she had remembered to load her briefcase with work before she left Tryad on Friday. She'd done it mostly out of habit, but now she was thankful; at least she could occupy her own mind with something productive. She certainly didn't have to entertain Logan. He could look after himself—as any roommate would be expected to, she told herself firmly.

But as her foot hit the last step, she heard herself saying, "I think there are some sweet rolls in the freezer. It's not much of a breakfast, but if you'd like—"

Logan bent to gather up the scattered sections of the newspaper. "It's a little late for breakfast, don't you think?"

She was annoyed, though for a moment she wasn't sure why. Because he'd rejected a civil, polite offer? Or was it the implied criticism of her layabout habits that had irritated her? "It's Sunday," she pointed out. "So what if I want to stay in bed till noon?"

He looked startled. "Did I sound as if I was scolding you?"

"As a matter of fact—"

"That's not at all what I meant. I was just thinking—"

"You know," Alison interrupted, "I'm beginning to get a cramp in my tummy every time you say that."

He smiled. "Don't panic. It's such a beautiful day, I thought you might want to go to the zoo. We could stop at one of the kiosks for a hot dog, and then—"

Alison stared at him. "The zoo?"

"You've heard of it?"

"I just didn't expect... You want to go to the zoo?"

"Well, somebody's got to do it—go wandering among the enclosures so the chimpanzees and giraffes and flamingos can have a laugh at all the funny humans. The animals would be lonely if nobody went and made fools of themselves on Sunday afternoons."

"And today's our turn?"

"I volunteer every now and then. It keeps me humble."

"I'd think it would take more than a chimpanzee to do that," Alison said under her breath.

She really did have work to do; the briefcaseful of papers wasn't just an excuse to fill her afternoon. But the sun spilling through the skylights called to her. There wouldn't be a great many more beautiful days before winter closed in.

"All right," she said. "Just let me run up and get a sweater."

The walk was a pleasant one; Alison hadn't noticed before that the chilly evenings had taken their toll and the leaves were beginning to turn. In the brilliant sunshine, the early traces of fall color glowed. They sauntered along at an easy pace, Logan with hands tucked in his pockets, Alison toying with the sleeves of the red sweater she'd slung casually around her shoulders.

The zoo wasn't as crowded as Alison had thought it might be, but there were young families everywhere she looked. Twin toddlers in a double stroller, a baby asleep in a backpack, a very pregnant woman with a stuffed whale tucked under her arm...

Alison tried not to look at any of them, and she thought she'd been successful until Logan said abruptly, "Maybe this wasn't such a good idea after all."

She followed his gaze to the rail of the nearest enclosure, where a man was holding a little girl up high so she could admire the sea lions frolicking in their pool. "It's all right," she said. "I'm not so self-centered that I can't be glad for other people, you know."

"Why—" He stopped abruptly, as if he'd caught himself in the nick of time, and took her arm to stroll toward a vendor. "I'm getting hungry. Are you?"

Alison wondered exactly what he'd been about to ask. There were so many possibilities, and each of them offered a completely different hint into the way his mind worked. She was so intrigued with the question that she didn't realize how much ketchup she'd put on her hot dog until she tried to bite into it and it shot out of the bun like a shell from a rocket launcher. She managed to catch it, and sat stock-still for an instant, bun in one hand, hot dog in the other, unable to do anything about the ketchup dripping from her chin.

Logan, she saw, was biting his lip hard, though it didn't seem to be helping much.

"I know," she said grumpily. "You don't understand why I think I need a kid when I act just like one."

Logan murmured, "Perhaps that's all the explanation necessary. But as long as you're admitting the resemblance, you *could* stand having your face washed." He put his hot dog down, pulled a white handkerchief from his pocket, and slid a finger under her chin to turn her face toward him.

Alison tried to fend him off. "If you spit on that handkerchief—"

"Your mother did that, too?" He wiped a streak of ketchup off her chin and draped the handkerchief over her knee like a napkin. "Just in case you need it again." He picked up his hot dog and added thoughtfully, "You *did* have a mother, then? And maybe a father, too?"

Alison fit her sandwich back together as best she could. "Of course. You don't think I sprang from a seashell like Venus, do you?"

"One could be allowed to wonder, since no one even showed up to walk you down the aisle—"

"I didn't want anyone. The custom of giving the bride away is a chauvinistic holdover from the Dark Ages."

"It's still a nice tradition," Logan argued.

Alison's gaze had wandered. Most of the people in view were different now; the toddlers in the stroller were gone, and the baby in the backpack was nowhere in sight. But sitting on a bench nearby was the pregnant woman she'd noticed earlier carrying the stuffed gray whale. Now there was a child beside her, a small girl who held a bright red helium balloon which bobbed up and down as she chattered. Alison couldn't catch the words, but she was vaguely irritated that the woman didn't seem interested. Instead, uncomfortable as the position must be, she had slumped down with her head resting on the back of the bench…

And she's looking very much as I must have, Alison thought, *during that last appendicitis attack.*

She'd hardly been listening to Logan, but she vaguely heard him say, "Besides, fair is fair, and you've met my parents."

"Believe me, you haven't missed anything." Alison's voice was abstracted. "Logan, that woman over there—"

He turned to look just as the woman stood up and gestured for the child to come to her. Then she doubled over.

Logan put his hot dog down on the handkerchief which was still draped across Alison's lap. He moved without apparent haste, but by the time she'd disentangled herself from the food and stood up, he was already beside the woman, easing her back onto the bench.

Alison pushed past a couple who'd stopped to stare. "Don't just stand there," she ordered. "Go look for a security guard or a zoo employee—or somebody who's got a cell phone." Bitterly regretting that she'd left her own portable recharging at home, she dropped to her knees beside the bench. "What can I do?"

"We're going to need an ambulance," Logan murmured, and Alison waved down the couple she'd dispatched and sent them running toward the main gate.

The woman's face was wrenched with pain and, Alison thought, a good share of embarrassment. "I thought I had plenty of time," she gasped. "And Chrissy wanted so much to come to her friend's birthday party..."

"When's the baby due?" Logan asked.

"Not till next week. And the pains didn't start till after we got here. I thought I'd just sit quietly till the party was done, and then walk home. It should be hours yet. Maybe if I rest a bit I can still—"

Alison didn't hear what Logan said, but she saw the way he shook his head.

A female security guard appeared at Alison's elbow. She was young, and the distress in her eyes warred with the confident set of her shoulders under her tailored uniform. "What's wrong? We've got an ambulance coming."

"Good," Alison said dryly. "Because it appears we're going to have a baby just about any minute."

The guard's eyes widened even more, and she fumbled for the radio hanging from her belt. "A baby? I've never..." Her voice faltered. "I don't know if the zoo vet's here today, but that's the best I can—"

Logan looked up. "It would do me a lot more good if you could locate some clean water and a lot of paper towels, and something to wrap a baby in." Without waiting to see if he was obeyed, he bent over his patient again.

The guard sped off. Alison untied the sleeves of her sweater and put it down beside him. "It's not much of a baby blanket," she said. "But it's better than nothing."

He said something she didn't quite hear, because in the same instant a bright red object bobbed up behind the bench and vanished again. *Oh, no*, she thought. *All of us forgot about the little girl. Chrissy—was that what her mother called her?*

The back of the bench was tall enough to conceal the child even if she'd been standing, and if it hadn't been for the red balloon Alison wouldn't have thought to look there for her. As it was, the child had sat down, a huddled little heap with one finger in her mouth and the balloon held close to her chest as if she drew comfort from its buoyancy.

Alison edged around the end of the bench and approached the little girl carefully. No doubt she'd been taught not to talk to strangers, so it wasn't going to be easy to break the ice, much less move her away from her mother.

Chrissy couldn't be more than four, Alison thought, and she was as wide-eyed and delicate as a fawn. She'd probably frighten just as easily, too.

"Chrissy," she said softly. "The doctor is going to take very good care of your mommy. Will you come over here a little way with me? We'll sit on the very next bench so you can see that she'll be just fine." *And far enough away that you won't see any more of the process itself than I can help,* Alison thought.

Chrissy stared at her for a full thirty seconds. Then she slowly took her finger out of her mouth and wrapped a still-damp hand around Alison's.

Alison sighed with relief at the trusting grasp. *She's only a baby herself,* she thought. "My name's Ali."

"But that's like a street," the child objected.

Alison laughed. "Well, it can be. But in this case it isn't." She arranged herself on the end of the bench to block Chrissy's view as much as possible while still letting her see that her mother hadn't disappeared. "Whose birthday party did you go to?"

Before long, Chrissy was sitting in Alison's lap. She showed Alison the penny she'd found on the zoo path, the knot which held her balloon to her wrist so it couldn't escape like the last one she'd had, and the scrape on her knee she'd gotten just yesterday when somebody named Tommy had pushed her.

But Alison was listening for something beyond Chrissy's conversation, and with each long and silent minute that went by her anxiety increased. What if the baby wasn't all right? What if it wasn't a normal birth? The situation was dreadful to begin with; could even Logan deal with all the complications which might arise? With no equipment, no help...

The infant arrived no more than a minute before the ambulance crew did; the baby's first astonished, protesting shriek was still resounding as the paramedics bustled down the path. But the strident cry was as relaxing as a lullaby to Alison. She was absolutely wrung out; she didn't want to imagine what the baby's mother must feel like.

Chrissy clapped her hands over her ears. "Is that the baby? It's loud!" She was almost yelling herself, as if in competition.

"In a few minutes you can go over and look at him—or her."

Chrissy looked perplexed. "Mommy said the baby would sleep a lot. She didn't say it'd yell."

Alison tried not to smile. "He will sleep a lot. But just now—"

"Just now," Logan said from just behind and above her, "he's not very happy with his new world, or with me for bringing him into it. How'd you know it's a boy, Alison? Feminine intuition?" He grinned at her and dropped to one knee beside the bench. "Chrissy, you're going to ride in the ambulance now with your mother and your little brother, and by the time you get to the hospital your father will be there waiting."

Chrissy frowned and said logically, "Mommy said she'd

go to the hospital to get the baby. But if she's already got him, why is she going to the hospital now?''

Alison's gaze met Logan's, and she had to bite her tongue to keep from responding to the laughter in his eyes.

They handed Chrissy over to the ambulance crew; she was disappointed to learn that there would probably be no siren running to make her ride more special. They said goodbye to her mother, who was teary with relief and gratitude. Alison touched the baby's still-wet dark curls with a gentle fingertip.

''He looks pretty good in your red sweater, don't you think?'' Logan asked.

As soon as the procession had left, the two of them collapsed once more on the bench where they'd been having lunch—at least a couple of aeons ago, Alison thought. She gathered up the dried-out fragments of her hot dog bun, deposited them in the nearest trash container, and neatly refolded Logan's ketchup-stained handkerchief.

Logan had stretched his feet out well into the path and closed his eyes. ''Thanks, Alison.''

Startled, Alison said, ''For what?''

''For one thing, I didn't need a four-year-old assistant.''

''Oh, well—anybody would have done that. What you did was the special part, Logan.''

He shrugged. ''Par for the course,'' he said, and yawned. ''It figures, though—I can't even take an entire weekend off to get married.''

The sun went under a cloud as they walked home, and the sudden chill in the air reminded Alison that she'd given up her favorite sweater. She shivered, and Logan draped an arm around her shoulders. The easy companionship the gesture displayed comforted her even more than his physical warmth.

''Before we were interrupted by an infant with no manners,'' he said, ''we were talking about families.''

Alison tried to keep herself from tensing. Why did he have to go and ruin things? "Were we?" She did her best to sound uninterested.

"And you indicated you had a family, but—"

"I—what? I didn't say—"

"You told me," Logan reminded, "that you didn't *want* anyone to walk you down the aisle. Not that you didn't *have* anyone to do the honors—or even to attend the wedding, which is what you told my mother over dinner the other night."

"Don't you think you're splitting hairs?"

"If you do have a family, don't you think I have some right to know? What if I come home from the hospital some day and discover that my in-laws have come to visit? It's going to be a little embarrassing if I don't have the cast of characters straight."

"Don't waste any sleep over it," Alison recommended. "Because it's never going to happen." She increased the pace. Logan let his arm drop from around her shoulders, but he stayed right beside her as they walked another block in silence.

"All right," Logan conceded. "You don't want to talk about it, and you're obviously stubborn enough that you wouldn't give in under torture. Am I at least allowed to know why having a baby is so important to you?"

"What's so unusual about a woman wanting a baby?"

"Nice dodge," he said admiringly. "But not good enough. It's the circumstances that are unusual, Alison. You don't appear to be a man-hater, but—"

"Thanks for that commendation," Alison said dryly. "Though what makes you think it's your business—" With relief, she saw the row house come into view. The thought of hot chocolate and a comfortable chair speeded up her pace even more. "I feel like I've just done a marathon."

"Have you ever had a good foot rub?"

A strange feeling—half wariness, half warmth—trickled through her at the thought of his hands, strong and skilled, massaging any part of her—even her feet. "No. And if you're offering—"

"I am. I'm told I'm rather good at it."

By whom? Alison wondered, and reminded herself that if her family—what there was of it—was not his concern, then the list of ladies who'd had their feet soothed was certainly not hers. "Thanks. But you've had a busy enough day without that."

He didn't answer, just reached for his key.

It was really kind of funny, Alison thought. She'd simply been tired before. Now, as though her body was responding to his suggestion, the arches of her feet had begun to ache.

The living room was no longer drenched in sunshine. In the dimness, the red light blinking on Alison's answering machine stood out like a lighthouse beacon. There were still plenty of her friends who hadn't yet heard about the wedding—or perhaps had heard by now and were calling up to give their reactions.

"I guess I'll just have to keep one finger on the *delete* button," she joked, "in case there are messages from all my old boyfriends."

The first call was Mrs. Sinclair, summoning—not inviting—them to dinner. Alison didn't even ask whether they had to go; Logan's sigh was answer enough.

The second was a voice she hadn't heard in months. "Alison? You know, you *could* call your mother once in a while…"

She pushed a button, and the mechanical voice of the machine said, "End of messages." She stood beside the machine, head bowed. *Of all the days,* she thought, *why this one?*

Logan looked over his shoulder. "That was it?"

"Oh, I'm sure she rambled on for quite some time." Her voice was tense.

"And you didn't even listen before erasing the message?"

Alison put her chin up. "Is there any particular reason you think it's your business?"

There wasn't a flicker of gold in his eyes, only hard dark green. "Just that I was beginning to think you weren't the kind of woman who would do that. Obviously I was wrong."

And just what did he know about it? she wanted to ask. But any answer at all would only invite further questions, and a discussion in which she had no wish to participate. One thing was sure: she didn't owe Logan any explanations.

She looked straight at him in silence.

He watched her for another long moment before he turned away. The sound of his footsteps on the hardwood floor echoed even after he'd taken a jacket from the closet beside the front door and gone out.

Only then did the trembling in her soul seep outward, till her entire body was shaking like an aspen tree in a March wind.

CHAPTER EIGHT

LOGAN didn't return, and by the time Alison was ready for bed she was starting to wonder if he was going to reappear at all. She hesitated as she checked the locks, even putting one hand on the security chain. If he wasn't coming back, she should fasten it; the house—and she—would be safer that way.

But she didn't click the chain into place.

She told herself she left it off purely because his key wouldn't open it, and she didn't want to be roused by the doorbell to let him in—any more than she'd want to get up in the middle of the night to admit any other housemate.

But she hadn't yet gone to sleep when she heard him come in, and the wave of relief which rolled over her was so strong it shocked her.

She lay there and thought it through. Of course she was glad he'd come back. If that one tiny dispute had been enough to derail their agreement, it wouldn't have said much for the strength of their bargain or the odds of their success. But in fact, they both had far too much at stake to let anything get in the way. Especially something which was so intensely personal, since their bargain emphatically was *not...*

By the time she'd worked out the logic, Alison had talked herself to sleep.

The sound of the guest room shower woke her the next morning, and she lay quietly, hugging a pillow, until she heard it turn off. *It's time to get up,* she told herself.

But she had to will herself to get out of bed, to go downstairs, to be ready to greet Logan as if nothing important had happened—because, she reminded, it hadn't. Logan had expressed an opinion, that was all—one based on incomplete information, and one she happened to disagree with.

He'd started a pot of coffee, and Alison was pouring herself a cup when he appeared around the corner from the guest room, hair still slightly damp, dressed for the day in navy trousers and a pale blue striped shirt. He stopped beside the breakfast bar as if he was surprised to see her there.

It was silly, Alison told herself, to feel trapped; he wasn't exactly blocking the way to the living room. And it was sillier yet to watch for even the slightest bit of interest in his gaze; in her long white terry cloth robe, she must look about as intriguing as a monk.

"I was thinking about bringing you a cup," Logan said, "and wondering if I'd get it wrapped around my head at this hour."

Alison reached for another mug. "It's Monday—Kit and Susannah and I always meet for breakfast to plan the week. And I like getting an early start to the day myself." She handed him the brimming mug.

"Except for Sundays, of course," Logan said. "About that phone call yesterday—"

Was he going to apologize for poking into her personal affairs? Alison turned a little away and reached for the coffeepot, topping off her cup so she didn't have to look straight at him. "What about it?"

"I'm afraid we'll have to accept the Sinclairs's dinner invitation—though maybe I can put the actual date off long enough that it won't matter anymore."

And what about the other phone call? Alison wanted to ask. Had he put that one out of his mind altogether? And wasn't that what she'd wanted him to do—since her dealings with her mother were emphatically none of Logan's affair?

"Until you find another job, you mean?" She kept her voice steady. "Do you have some good prospects already?"

Logan shrugged. "Nothing solid yet. It'll take a bit of time, especially since I can't exactly come straight out and tell everyone I run into that I'm looking for a change. But I put out some feelers last week, and I think it's promising."

"That's good. Keep me posted, all right?"

"Of course. In the meantime, I'll call Mrs. Sinclair and try to stall. You probably have something scheduled every weekend for the next month—don't you?"

"No doubt. Or if not, I'll find something." Alison picked up a few dirty dishes from the sink and loaded them into the dishwasher. "But I suspect she'd think it was far more socially appropriate for me to do the calling, don't you, instead of leaving it to the busy doctor? That way I can plead the need to check with you before scheduling a particular date."

Logan grinned. "And have one more reason for delay. You may be onto something there."

Alison dumped the rest of her coffee down the drain. "I'd better get moving." The last thing she wanted was to be late this morning. She seemed to remember making a few sly comments about her partners' inability to function at a normal level in the first week or two after their respective honeymoons, so she shouldn't be surprised at getting a little innuendo back. She didn't have to provide them with ammunition, however.

"See you tonight, then, but I don't have any idea when I'll be finished."

Alison rinsed her cup and put it in the dishwasher. "If that's a polite way to tell me not to delay dinner for you, you may as well know that I hadn't intended to."

"I'm glad we understand one another." He moved aside

to let her pass through to the living room, and said as she brushed past, "Alison…where your mother's concerned—"

She froze in midstep. It wasn't fair, she thought, to let her think he'd forgotten all about that phone message yesterday and then blindside her when she least expected it. She didn't turn around to look at him, and her voice was not only level but icy. "I don't owe you any explanations, Logan."

"Absolutely right," he said. "That's what I wanted to tell you—I had no business interfering. I guess I was just putting my nose in everyone's affairs yesterday, wasn't I?"

He sounded almost cheerful about it, Alison thought. And she was pleased that instead of lecturing her once more on a subject he knew nothing about, he was taking such a rational approach. Wasn't she?

Alison was dead on time for the partners' regular breakfast meeting. But still she was the last to arrive; Kit and Susannah were already sitting in the back booth of the little restaurant just around the corner from Tryad's brownstone, and they'd obviously been there for a while. When Alison slid into her place on the bench, Kit was holding up a triangle of dry toast and looking with disfavor at Susannah's vegetarian omelette. Without even glancing at Alison, she extended her other hand across the table. "Pay up, Sue," she ordered.

Susannah grumbled, but she put her fork down and dug into her handbag.

"What's the bet?" Alison asked. She reached for the coffeepot and the last empty cup.

"Whether you'd show up at all this morning. Susannah, the fearless romantic, swore you wouldn't."

"So now I'm looking for a way to win my ten dollars

back," Susannah said. "Let's see… It's obvious that you've already had coffee, so nobody will bet on that."

"What's obvious about it?" Alison cradled her cup in both hands and told the waitress she'd like a blueberry muffin.

"Because you're sipping that cup," Susannah said, "which means it must be at least your second. Don't tell me—Logan brought you coffee in bed before he left for the hospital."

"Good thing you married a man with money, Sue, because you'd lose that bet, too." Just an instant too late, Alison saw the glint in Susannah's eyes.

"He didn't? How very unromantic of him. But it wasn't his bedside manner I was betting on, exactly."

"That's good. Because he would have brought my coffee if I hadn't already been up. Though why I rushed around to get here for this sort of discussion, when we have loads of business to talk about—"

Susannah obviously wasn't listening. "Kitty, I'll not only go double or nothing on the ten bucks I just lost, but I'll give you odds on this one. Logan didn't bring her the morning paper, either."

Kit shook her head. "What kind of fool do you think I am, Sue? Of course he didn't."

As a matter of fact, Alison had tripped over the newspaper on her way out the door, picked it up, and tossed it onto the foyer table, still neatly folded. "Why are you so sure?"

"Because if you already knew that you're the main feature in the society gossip column in the Metro section this morning, you wouldn't be sitting there so calmly." Susannah snapped her briefcase open and pulled out the newspaper, already folded back to display the column.

The waitress set a steaming muffin in front of Alison. She pushed it aside and grabbed for the paper. Images of yesterday's episode in the zoo chased each other through her mind. There had been dozens of people standing around by the time the whole thing was over; why hadn't it occurred to her that the incident was too good not to repeat? And of course it would eventually reach the ears of the gossip columnists, who thrived on oddball stories…

But it wasn't as bad as she had feared. In fact, there was nothing in the paper about the zoo at all; instead, the columnist had written a sly little item about the Singles club organizer who'd showed up late to the second meeting because she'd spent the afternoon marrying one of the club members.

Funny, Alison thought. *So much has happened since then, I'd forgotten all about the Singles club fiasco.*

And she wasn't the main feature, either, no matter how Susannah had made it sound. It was only a paragraph located toward the end of the column. Her name was prominent, but Logan's was barely mentioned—and the Chicago Singles might actually get some good publicity from it. Relieved, she handed the newspaper back to Susannah. "It could be worse."

"That's right," Kit said. "It could indeed be worse. I'll bet you didn't turn on the television, either."

"I never watch the morning shows unless one of you is going to be on. Oh, no—"

"They're calling it The Zoo Baby," Susannah murmured.

"It's a cute story, too," Kit agreed. "All about how the baby baboons and zebras—or whatever they have in the nursery just now—found themselves upstaged yesterday by another species of Zoo Baby."

"Oh, no."

"Complete with pictures," Susannah added gently. "One of the television stations happened to be filming something else at the zoo, and they managed to catch—"

"Oh, no."

Susannah asked tartly, "Ali, is there anything else in your vocabulary besides 'Oh, no'?"

"Not that I can say in public." Alison shook her head a little, but her brain didn't clear.

"They were shooting from a distance," Kit said, "so at least it doesn't pass for a medical documentary. But Logan was unmistakable. You looked a bit dishevelled, Ali, but he—"

"*I* was in this?"

"Oh, yes. They make quite a thing of you soothing the big sister. The story's three full minutes long, Ali—and they've been running it at least once an hour."

Alison put her hand over her eyes. Three minutes was an eternity in television—and three minutes out of each hour was unheard of. The President didn't get that kind of time unless he was dealing with a national emergency.

It wouldn't be long, she thought, before the gossip column people happened to turn on the TV features, and the television people picked up the newspaper and glanced at the gossip column. And once they put two and two together, then everyone in Chicago would know that not only had she and Logan done a good deed yesterday, but they had interrupted their honeymoon for it.

The honeymoon that had included spending the first full day of their marriage…at the zoo. Wouldn't people like Mrs. Sinclair have fun with that?

You'd better hope she does, Alison thought grimly. *Because if she isn't laughing, she'll be wondering.* And if Mrs. Sinclair started asking embarrassing questions about the state of the Kavanaugh's new marriage, everything they had tried to accomplish might be at stake. Logan's job would be even more at risk. And as for Alison's baby…

There's no reason that should be affected, she thought stubbornly. It wasn't Alison's fault the woman had been at the zoo when she needed help. And Alison certainly hadn't invited the television crew to participate. It hadn't even been her idea to go to the zoo in the first place.

But if Logan's job was yanked out from under him after all, Alison could hardly expect that her part of the bargain would be the top item on his priority list.

She didn't realize she was on her feet until Susannah said, "If you're headed over to the office, you might want to take this." She held up a videotape. "I taped the story so you wouldn't have to waste time waiting through the whole news cycle to see yourself."

Kit reached into her handbag and pulled out another cassette. "So did I. And we can always call the station to ask for a really good copy for your portfolio—"

Alison swore under her breath and headed for Tryad's brownstone. She was hurrying up the sidewalk when she realized that Mrs. Holcomb was sitting on her own front steps, just a few feet from Tryad's porch—sitting still, for once, instead of hurrying away at the mere sight of another human being.

Alison's steps slowed.

Mrs. Holcomb's dark, beady gaze roved over Alison from head to foot, and then her face seemed to collapse under an entirely new set of wrinkles, until only her eyes looked the same.

Mrs. Holcomb, Alison realized, was smiling.

"I saw you on television," she said. "So that young man of yours is a doctor, hmm? Right nice to have a doctor around."

Three sentences in a row? Alison was practically in shock. "Well—sometimes. I mean, *yes*."

"Take care of him," Mrs. Holcomb advised. Her gaze slid past Alison toward the street, where several children were noisily wending their way to school, and she pushed herself up from the step and retreated like a wraith behind her solid front door.

Alison shook her head and climbed the steps to Tryad.

The door was already unlocked, the scent of fresh coffee filled the air, and Rita was standing at the copy machine in her office. "Just in case you haven't seen the story, I set the television cart up in the conference room," she said. "The tape's already in and cued."

"You made a copy, too?" Alison glanced down at the two black plastic cases she held. "Though to tell the truth, the only thing that surprises me is that Mrs. Holcomb didn't." She started toward the conference room.

"She probably did, but she just didn't want to give it away," Rita said. "Oh, one more thing, Alison—I forgot to ask what name you're going to use."

"Has something gone wrong with the one I have?"

"Then when the reporters start calling for Mrs. Kavanaugh, you want me to correct them?"

Alison sighed. If this was honestly a marriage, she'd keep her own name and not give a thought to anyone else's opinion. She'd established herself professionally as Alison Novak, and she'd be darned if she'd start over. But under the circumstances, the last thing she wanted was to give anyone even the tiniest of reasons to question her commitment to the marriage…

"No," she said. "What difference does it make what they call me?" She didn't wait for an answer, and she closed the golden oak sliding doors between Rita's office and the conference room before she turned on the television set. Her palms were damp with morbid anticipation by the time the tape started to play.

Kit was right; the story was cute. In fact, it positively dripped cuteness. Professionally photographed and sharply edited, it was a story that had everything going for it—a cliff-hanger of a situation featuring a handsome hero, set against a background of cuddly, awkward baby animals, and coming to a warm-fuzzy of an ending as mother, baby and big sister rode off into the sunset—or something like that. The only thing missing was romance...except it wouldn't be missing for long.

"We'll be lucky," Alison muttered, "if we can keep it from jumping into the national news."

She was slumped in her chair staring at the blank television screen when Rita tapped on the door. "Alison? Dr. Kavanaugh's on the phone."

She took the call at Rita's desk, picking up the telephone as carefully if it were molten steel.

Logan's voice was cheerful. "You'll never guess what my first patient brought me."

"Let me think," Alison said dryly. "Could it maybe be—a videotape?"

"You already heard?"

"I not only heard, I've seen. Logan, in all the years I've been in public relations, I've never known *anybody* to get this kind of coverage."

"So next time you see a very pregnant woman in obvious distress, don't point her out to me."

Alison's jaw dropped. "It wasn't exactly my idea—well, yes, I guess it was, wasn't it?"

"At least half. That wasn't the main reason I called, though. From something Burt let drop this morning, I think Mrs. Sinclair is planning on dinner next Saturday. I figured if you knew ahead of time—"

Alison was nodding. "I could already be prepared with an excuse. Actually... You said Saturday? I don't need an excuse, because I've got a good reason. That's the night my video premieres."

"I thought it already had."

"Not the Zoo Baby, Logan, the promotional tape I've

been working on for the last year. Chicago—what a great place it is to live and work, things like that.''

"I didn't know you were a film star.''

"I'm not. I just produced the thing—and if I'd had any idea what I was getting into, I'd have charged them triple.''

"And it's next Saturday? I'll make sure I've got the night off.''

"Really, there's no need, Logan. I mean, you'd hate it—it'll be one of those deadly dull banquets featuring rubbery chicken and a boring speaker. You don't have to go.''

"And miss my wife's debut as a film director? Alison, my dear—what kind of husband do you think I am?'' A note of anxiety crept into his voice; Alison was fairly sure it was deliberate. "Though you *will* make sure there aren't any past-due pregnant people allowed in—won't you?''

Alison would have hung up on him if he hadn't beat her to the draw.

She stacked her collection of Zoo Baby videotapes neatly on the corner of her desk and settled down with her list of things to do. *Get the hardest out of the way first,* she told herself. It had been her rule—and a good one it was, too—for years.

But when she glanced at the clock she decided that perhaps it would be even wiser in this case to start with the second hardest item, so she dialed the Sinclairs's number. She almost choked as she identified herself; *Alison Kavanaugh* sat uncomfortably on her tongue.

"I'm simply amazed,'' Mrs. Sinclair said, "that you've had time to call.''

Well, I knew better than to hope she might not have seen it, Alison told herself. She was a bit annoyed, however, at the level of sarcasm in Mrs. Sinclair's voice. The woman sounded as scandalized as if it had been Alison herself who'd given birth in a public park.

"The woman was in distress,'' Alison said, "so we did

what we could to help. We had no idea there was a television crew within miles.''

''The woman,'' Mrs. Sinclair said flatly, ''was a fool. And so was Dr. Kavanaugh. In today's litigious climate, any doctor who steps into the middle of a mess like that—a patient he's never seen, a pregnancy he knows nothing about—is asking to be sued. If something goes wrong...''

Alison could actually feel the hairs rising on the back of her neck, as if she was a cat protecting her young. ''Things would have been a lot more likely to go wrong if Logan hadn't stepped in.''

Mrs. Sinclair didn't seem to hear. ''And with a videotape as evidence, too... Perhaps I should mention to Doctor Sinclair that it might be time for a review session with all the partners.''

Alison said sharply, ''To review what? How to smother their consciences and walk on by?'' She caught herself; snapping at the senior partner's wife was hardly any way to smooth Logan's path—and just now the last thing he needed was for Alison to be throwing rocks in his way. Besides, she consoled herself, there was no point in wasting breath; nothing she could say would convince Mrs. Sinclair that she was stupid and cruel and heartless.

''There are certain practicalities in the modern world,'' Mrs. Sinclair said complacently. ''But of course that wasn't why I called. Dr. Sinclair and I will expect you and Dr. Kavanaugh Saturday at eight for dinner. A chance to get acquainted, you know.''

That isn't an invitation, Alison thought, *it's a summons.* ''I'm sorry,'' she said, ''but Saturday won't work for me. I have a business conflict.''

''A business conflict? My dear girl, your business— whatever it is—can hardly be as important as your husband's practice.''

''It is to me,'' Alison said firmly. ''So I'm afraid we'll

have to decline your very kind invitation and hope that another time we'll be able to accept.''

Mrs. Sinclair didn't offer an alternative date. Alison didn't know whether to panic or be relieved. She'd certainly succeeded in putting the woman off—but had she done too good a job?

Well, she certainly wasn't going to waste time worrying about it now, when she had a million other things to do.

The moment she put the telephone down the intercom buzzed. ''Alison, there's a woman from *Chicago Morning* on line two, wanting to schedule you on the show, and a man from the newspaper on line three—''

''I think I just went out for a conference,'' Alison suggested. ''And I might not be back for a week or more.''

She looked down at her list. It was a strange feeling, she thought, to know that she'd rather call her mother than talk to a bunch of piranha-like reporters.

The telephone rang a dozen times before a sleep-slurred voice growled, ''Who the hell is this?''

''You did suggest that I call,'' Alison said crisply.

''Well, I didn't *suggest* that you do it in the middle of the night!''

Alison checked her wristwatch and added an hour. ''It's half past ten in the morning in Florida, Mother. What did you want?''

''Didn't you listen to my message?''

''Yes, I did.'' Twice, in fact, after Logan had walked out, before she'd finally wiped it out of the answering machine's memory. ''I understand that you're still a bit upset with my father, but as for the rest—''

Alison might as well have lit a stick of dynamite. She held the phone several inches from her ear until her mother had finished describing the man in question, in vivid detail and X-rated language.

''I don't know what you think I can do about it,'' Alison

said finally. "You'd been divorced from him for twenty years when he died, so I can't quite see why you should expect him to have left you anything at all in his will."

"*He* divorced *me*," her mother whined.

Alison told herself there was no point in reminding her mother exactly why the marriage had ended.

"And married that..." The blue language started to flow.

Alison gritted her teeth, since some of her mother's opinions of the woman who had been her father's second wife came uncomfortably close to her own.

"And she collected every cent of his estate," her mother finished triumphantly. "It's not fair."

"Perhaps not, but he had a right to leave his property as he chose. There's not much I can do about it."

"You can sue to overturn the will. You should have had a share."

Which you would then demand as your rightful due for bringing me into the world, Alison thought. "We've been over all this before, Mother. I'm not going to do anything."

She listened to only a few of the adjectives her mother used to describe her before she put the telephone down, firmly cutting off the stream of invective.

Her hands were shaking. They almost always did, after a cozy little chat with her mother.

She opened the drawer of her desk where all of her current projects were stored and took out the first of them. Burying herself in work was the best answer, she'd found. It always made the pain go away...eventually.

Alison had said she had no intention of keeping dinner hot for Logan, and she'd meant it. Even if this has been a real marriage, she couldn't quite picture herself playing the little housewife in a frilly, spotless apron, waiting by the door with his slippers in hand no matter when he came home.

Nevertheless, he wasn't the only one who had to eat once

in a while—and with the day she'd had, she was craving comfort food. So she stopped at the market on her walk home, more to browse for something that sounded good than to buy anything in particular. But the bin of fresh tomatoes by the front door called out to her. They were home-grown ones, irregular in shape, widely varied in size—but rich red, juicy, and fragrant. The sharp scent of them made her think of marinara sauce, thick and rich and spicy, filling the house with fragrance.

The fact that the longer it simmered the tastier it would be wasn't a consideration at all.

She had just finished chopping the tomatoes and was adding the first round of spices to the kettle when the telephone rang. She gave a last stir to the sauce and reached for the phone, but there was no one on the line, just silence and then a soft click.

Probably just a prank call, she told herself. But silent hang-ups could be worrisome; burglars sometimes phoned a house they were staking out, to see if it was empty. Well, if it rang again she wouldn't answer—and in the meantime, she'd make sure every lock was fastened, just in case.

It was almost half an hour before the next call. She kept on stirring her sauce and let the phone ring, but when the answering machine picked up a vaguely familiar feminine voice said, "Alison? I don't mean to trouble you. It's Camilla Kavanaugh—"

Alison grabbed for the phone, burning herself on the kettle in the process. "Hi. Sorry, I was—" She paused. If she told the truth, she'd leave Logan's mother with the impression that she was Little Miss Homemaker, which was about as far from reality as it was possible to get. It was an interesting ethical dilemma, she thought. Tell the truth, which was misleading? Or tell a lie, which in the long run was closer to reality?

"My dear, don't ever feel you have to interrupt anything

to talk to me," Camilla said. "Or explain anything, either. Two people as busy as you and Logan are—finding time for each other will be enough of a challenge, I'm afraid, without feeling you have to jump if I happen to call."

"Umm…well, yes." Alison felt bemused. There wasn't a hint of irony in Camilla's voice; Alison felt a little guilty nevertheless.

"I won't keep you, my dear. But I've just found out that Logan's father and I will be in Chicago again over the weekend, and we wondered if we could take the two of you out for dinner on Saturday night."

Now that, Alison thought, was an invitation she could almost enjoy—the key word being *almost*—if it wasn't for the video premiere. "I'm so sorry, but I'm afraid—"

"You have plans," Camilla said. "Of course. We understand completely."

On the other hand, Alison thought, *let's kill two birds with one stone, shall we?* "I'm committed that evening, but Logan doesn't have to go, and I'm sure he'd much prefer dinner with you to a dull banquet."

"It's sweet of you to be so generous, Alison, but we'd really like to see you both."

"Well, I'm sure sometime during the weekend… Where will you be staying?"

Camilla said smoothly, "At the Drake, as we usually do."

But had there been a millisecond of silence, the smallest hesitation, before she'd answered? Alison's heart dropped to her toes. *In normal situations,* she told herself, *people stay with family, not in hotels.*

She heard her own voice, disastrously firm and assertive, saying, "Not this time. You must come to us, I insist."

Camilla chatted for a couple of minutes more, and then Alison put the phone down and sank onto the nearest chair.

And just how, she thought, *am I going to explain this to Logan?*

Temporary insanity, she decided. It seemed the only thing which fit.

The doorbell rang, startling her for an instant before she remembered that she'd fastened all the dead bolts and chains, and Logan was probably wondering why his key wouldn't open the door. She hurried to answer it.

But it wasn't Logan who stood on the front step; it was a milling mass of people who in one breath shouted "Surprise!" and burst over the threshold into the living room. There were probably no more than two dozen of them, but Alison would have sworn her house had been invaded by a Mongol horde.

In the lead was her friend Jake, the one who always had a funny story, waving a champagne bottle. "We felt left out," he announced. "You didn't even throw an engagement party for your friends—so we decided to do it ourselves. So everybody brought food, and we gathered over at Sherry's and called to be certain you were home before we came." He grinned. "We do hope we're not interrupting anything…interesting."

Alison laughed. "You're a liar, too, Jake. Come on in—though since you're *already* in, I can hardly throw you out. One of me against all of you…"

"Relax and enjoy it," Jake recommended. He started to tear the foil from the champagne bottle. "Glasses still in the kitchen?"

"Where else?" Alison asked. "And turn the heat off under my marinara sauce while you're there."

The party was as uproarious as any Alison had ever attended; the only thing missing was the groom. Which wasn't the same thing at all, she told herself, as saying that she *missed* him…

In fact, she didn't even see him come in. They'd rolled

up the rugs by then, and she was dancing with Jake when the noise level suddenly dropped and heads turned toward the front door.

She stopped dancing in midstep, still in Jake's arms.

Logan was standing just inside the door, forehead wrinkled slightly, eyes roving the crowd.

Alison's heart started to pound, thudding painfully against her ribs. She couldn't seem to get a full breath. Did he think this was her normal after-work behavior? What would he have to say about finding her in another man's arms? Should she even try to explain, or toss her head and pretend it didn't matter what he thought?

If so, she would have to pretend—because it *did* matter. The realization hit her with the weight of a rock slide.

Logan came across the room, each step slow and deliberate, until he was less than two feet away.

"Uh—" Jake said. He sounded so uneasy he was almost breathless. "You're not upset, are you?"

For a moment it seemed Logan hadn't heard him. He was watching Alison. She couldn't meet his gaze, so she focused on the tiny white scar on his lip.

"Upset?" he said softly. "How can I be, when Alison has such good taste in friends?" He moved just a little closer. "However, as long as we're having a party, I'd like to dance with my wife. You won't take it personally, will you, Jake?"

Jake almost stumbled in his eagerness to get clear. Somebody started the music again, and Logan drew her close. Alison closed her eyes.

The slightest scent of cologne still clung to him, mixed in an oddly attractive combination with a hint of hospital antiseptic. Her body felt like jelly, melting against his warmth. The strength of his arms provided the framework she needed to stay upright; her bones no longer could.

And as she settled into his arms, comprehension pierced

her mind like a flaming arrow, and she knew why it mattered so much to her what he thought of the party, of her friends, of her conduct. *Of her.*

She knew now why she'd felt that rush of softness when he was there at the chapel door, waiting for her. It hadn't been simple gratitude she felt.

She understood why it had hurt so much yesterday when he'd assumed she was a heartless, thankless child for not wanting to talk to her mother.

She recognized why she'd felt so relieved last night when he'd came back after their disagreement...

She'd constructed complicated, logical explanations for each of her reactions at the time. But those complex justifications hadn't been the real reasons.

In fact, there was only one reason. It was elegantly simple, and absolutely devastating. She'd been grateful, concerned, upset, and relieved not for all the logical reasons she'd given herself...but because she loved him.

CHAPTER NINE

THE entire idea was utterly and absolutely crazy—but that didn't make it any less real. And Alison, who had learned almost from babyhood that facing facts straight out hurt less in the long run than denying them, stared this truth in the eye and surrendered to it.

Sometime in the course of the last few weeks, she had fallen in love with Logan Kavanaugh. She didn't know how it had happened, or when—and perhaps it didn't matter. Understanding the process wouldn't make the facts go away. Now the question was what she was going to do about it.

Nothing, she told herself. There was nothing she could do; she could hardly change the terms of their agreement now.

And even if she could, would she want to? Admitting that she'd grown to love him was one thing—but it didn't necessarily follow that she was desperate to link her whole future with his. All her reasons for not wanting to share her life, her child with any man were just as valid today as they'd been when she first enunciated them to Logan. Just because she'd come to care for him, it didn't mean she'd lost all her common sense.

And it's just as well, too, she told herself tartly, for she wasn't the only one with the power to make choices.

Alison drifted through the rest of the party in a sort of daze. When the revelers gathered up the debris and called it a night, she stood in the doorway to say goodbye.

"Boy, have you got it bad," one of the women murmured as she hugged Alison. "The minute that handsome hunk walked in the door, the rest of us might as well have disappeared in a puff of smoke.''

Alison felt herself coloring and hoping the handsome hunk in question hadn't overheard that.

Her guests had done a good job of clearing away the mess they'd made, but here and there a glass, a paper plate, a napkin had escaped notice. Alison picked up the last few things, plumped the crumpled cushions on the sofa, pulled a couple of chairs back into place. As she finished the cats reappeared, yawning and obviously relieved that the confusion was over.

Logan was in the kitchen assembling a sandwich from the leftover snacks. ''That was quite the party,'' he said as she came in. ''Do you have them often?''

''If you're wondering why you weren't invited, don't feel left out. Neither was I.'' She dipped a taco chip into a bowl of salsa and munched on it as she tried to figure out how to fit the kettle of marinara sauce into the refrigerator.

''Well, that's a relief—unless they make a habit of this sort of thing.''

Alison shook her head. ''This was strictly one of a kind.'' She gave up on finding a spot for the kettle and started looking instead for other containers to hold the sauce.

''Want half of my sandwich?''

''No, thanks. I've been nibbling all evening.''

Logan drizzled barbecue sauce over the thin-sliced beef piled in his sandwich. ''How'd you do with Mrs. Sinclair?''

''Actually, I may have done too good a job at putting her off. She seems to think because I won't give up my plans for yours that I'm the original liberated woman.''

''Well, I didn't expect that you'd be bosom buddies.'' Logan gathered up the sandwich.

''*Buddies?* I can't imagine agreeing with the woman about anything. She was absolutely vile, Logan. She actually suggested that you shouldn't have helped that poor woman for fear she'd turn around and sue you if…if her baby had less hair than she thought it should, or something equally stupid.''

''Really? That attitude must have made for an interesting conversation at the Sinclairs' dinner table tonight.''

''Why?''

''Because Burt thinks the whole thing was wonderful. He stopped just short of believing that you'd arranged the entire episode to make the practice look good.''

''What a compliment,'' Alison said faintly.

''Not really. He saved all the acclaim for himself, since he was the one who brought a PR consultant into it.''

''I thought it was your idea originally.''

''I wasn't about to remind him.'' He set the sandwich down and reached into the refrigerator for a soda. ''Maybe you should send him a bill for services rendered and bring him back down to earth.''

''Take credit for that? No, thanks. What I really can't believe is that Mrs. Sinclair honestly thought you should have left that woman alone and in pain—and almost certain to have complications—rather than take the faintest chance.''

Logan shrugged. ''To give the devil her due, things like that happen now and then.''

''But you wouldn't walk away.'' The firm phrasing was the farthest thing possible from a question. ''You couldn't.''

He looked at her for a long moment, and his face lit with a slow smile which seemed to reach deep inside her and twist each nerve as tight as a spring.

Hastily Alison turned her attention back to the marinara sauce. *Hang on to your common sense,* she told herself. *You're going to need it before this ride is over.*

* * *

She was fine as long as she was at work; Alison had no trouble occupying her mind every minute that she was at Tryad. In a matter of days, the video promotion which had occupied so much of her time and energy over the last year would be revealed to an audience of the most prominent and influential people in the city of Chicago. And though a single project couldn't make or break a career—or a company—Alison knew this one was important enough to make a serious dent not only in her reputation but in Tryad's if it was a flop.

It wouldn't be, of course. The video was darned good. But was it quite good enough? Was there one last thing somewhere which could be improved? One detail which had been overlooked?

And even after there could be absolutely no more changes made in the final master, there were nagging questions. Had everyone who should see the video been invited to the banquet? Were they all coming? Should she telephone the most important ones with a personal follow-up, or would that make it look as if they were having trouble gathering enough interested people to bother with the show?

Meanwhile, her row house was no longer the refuge that it had once been. The pressure there was different, but it was just as real. In fact, it was worse—because just being around Logan was enough to set her on edge. Behaving as though nothing had changed, when in fact she was so aware of his every breath that she ached, was the most difficult challenge she'd ever faced.

Why had she never before noticed, Alison wondered, that *acting natural* was a contradiction in terms?

The casual way he treated her didn't help. After a couple of mornings when he brought her coffee upstairs and sat for a few minutes on the side of her bed to chat, Alison made sure she was always up and dressed well before he was ready to leave. But that wasn't a great deal of improvement; in the small kitchen, it was hard to stay out of each other's way, and the merest brush of his body was enough to set off explosions in every cell he touched.

And when she avoided any possibility of physical contact by sitting in the living room instead, drinking her coffee and pretending to read the newspaper until it was time for him to go to work, she found herself feeling chilly, lonely, forlorn.

It was like riding a pendulum from one extreme to the other—and no matter which end of the swing she found herself on, she had to try to appear normal, completely unconcerned. At least at Tryad, everyone expected her to be absentminded and a bit short-tempered. But if she appeared that way to Logan, she was in no position to field the uncomfortable questions which might result.

She'd told him about his parents coming to Chicago for the weekend, but it wasn't until Friday morning that she worked up her nerve to add that she'd invited them to stay at the house. She was spooning coffee into the filter basket as she spoke, and he was filling the pot with water.

From the corner of her eye she saw that he'd gone rigid. Water filled the reservoir and spilled over, drenching the cuff of his shirt, before he recalled himself and turned off the faucet. But his voice was mild. "Why did you do that?"

Because I'm developing a real fondness for pain, she wanted to say. *I must be, the way I'm seeking it out.*

"I thought if I didn't it would seem suspicious. As if we had something to hide." Her voice was a shade higher and just a little faster than normal, but at least she didn't sound as if she was about to panic.

"And we don't? Have something to hide, I mean."

"Look, Logan, I didn't exactly have a chance to think it over. It—just happened." She took a deep breath. "Sort of like your announcement to Burt Sinclair that we were engaged.''

His eyebrows lifted quizzically.

Got you on that one, didn't I? Alison thought triumphantly. ''I'm sure if you had it to do over again, and another couple of minutes to think—''

''I see your point. And precisely how are you planning to manage this?''

''It's only one night, Logan. You'll have to move some things out of the guest room, of course. Not everything—I mean, don't you think it would be pretty normal for you to be using the downstairs closets?''

''I'd never given it a moment's contemplation. And just where am I to put these things I move?''

He wasn't about to make this easier, was he? Alison cleared her throat. ''I thought—we'll just have to share my room.''

''Oh, absolutely. Why not? It's far from the most enthusiastic invitation I've ever had to join a lady in her bed, but—''

Alison's face flamed. ''I am not inviting you to...to...''

''You can't even get your tongue around the words, can you?'' Logan sounded honestly curious. ''Don't worry. I know exactly what you mean—and what you don't mean, too. But I'm not the one who created this problem, Alison, and if you think *I'm* going to take a pillow into your bathtub and call it a bed, you're dead wrong.'' He pushed the coffeepot into place under the drip filter and went out to get the morning paper from the front step.

Alison couldn't have uttered a word, even if he'd given her the opportunity; her throat was frozen solid. Besides, she asked herself, what else was left to say?

Camilla Kavanaugh loved the row house. She loved the style in which Alison had decorated it. She loved the neighborhood, the way the sunlight drenched the flaming red maple that stood by the street, and the pot of vegetable soup that Alison produced for Saturday's lunch.

Alison was completely bemused; she couldn't catch a hint of exaggeration, much less untruth, in Camilla's attitude. Could the woman be real? It appeared so, and Alison was still off balance that evening as she dressed for the banquet at which the video would premiere.

She was fastening a dangling diamond earring—borrowed from Kit for the occasion—when the bedroom door opened and Logan came in. Startled, she wheeled to face him and dropped the earring. It skittered across the hardwood floor and under the edge of the bed.

Logan bent to retrieve it. As he handed back the glittering bauble, the tips of his fingers brushed her palm with flame. ''If you're wondering why I'm here, it's because Mom sent me up. Something about showing my support on this important occasion by at least zipping your dress.''

She might have known it wouldn't be his idea. Well, she didn't want that kind of complication, did she?

Alison shrugged as she secured the earring, sending the diamonds into a frenzy of brilliant sparks. The sequins which dripped over the bodice and sleeves of her black gown caught the light in a slightly more subdued fashion. ''It's already zipped.''

''I see. In a bit of a hurry, aren't you? Or is this a very early banquet?''

''No—the dinner doesn't start till eight. But I want to get there before the guests start to arrive, so I have plenty of time to check the equipment without giving anyone an unintentional sneak preview.''

''I thought perhaps you were anxious to get away before I came upstairs to change.''

That, too, Alison admitted, but she wasn't about to confess it to him. Her bedroom had never felt so small as it had this morning when he'd brought up his clothes, his shaving kit, his toothbrush. She couldn't imagine being there as he moved possessively around the room, fastening cuff links and bow tie and cummerbund...

But of course he wasn't going to be putting on formal attire; he was going out to dinner with his parents, not to Alison's banquet.

And I'm glad, she reminded herself.

He was standing almost directly behind her, looking over her shoulder into the mirror above her dressing table. Even wearing the highest heels she owned, and with her hair upswept, she felt small and fragile next to him. Or was part of that impression simply the contrast between her sleek, slim-fitting evening gown and the casual, bulky sweater he was wearing?

She picked up the necklace which matched the diamond earrings and held it up to her throat.

"Even if I'm too late to zip, I can fasten," Logan said, and his fingertips brushed the nape of her neck as he reached for the dainty ornament.

She wasn't prepared, and before she could stop herself Alison had pulled away. She saw curiosity spring to life in his eyes and said hastily, "I think the necklace is a little too much with all the sequins." She dropped it back into the box and met his gaze in the mirror. "Thanks anyway."

"I've been thinking," he said abruptly.

Alison let her perfectly arched eyebrows climb and said in mock horror, "Logan, you *thinking* is enough to strike terror into the heart of the entire United Nations."

He didn't seem to share the humor. "I should go to the premiere with you."

"And leave your parents on their own? Don't be silly. You can't just dump them at the last minute." She tugged one tendril of hair into place and turned to face him with a smile. "It's lovely of you, really, to volunteer to eat rubbery chicken and sit through a boring after-dinner speech, but it's decided. Where are you taking your parents? Cicero's?''

"Do you think they'd like it?''

"I think," Alison said frankly, "that your mother would like it even if you only took her out for popcorn. Is she for real?''

"I think the word is down-to-earth.''

"Yeah. Well, pardon me if it takes me a little while to adjust. In my profession, I don't see much of that.''

"Or in your life?'' Logan asked gently.

Her head snapped up. "I don't know what you mean.''

"Don't you?'' He reached out as if to touch her cheek, and flicked the dangling earring instead.

The tiny tug at her earlobe felt like a caress. "Speaking of professions," she said, "I haven't had a chance to ask how the job hunt is going. Weren't you going to talk to someone this morning?''

Logan nodded. He drew back his hand, and the soft note vanished from his voice. "I did. There's nothing certain, but he knew of a couple of possibilities. And he's in a better place to put out feelers than I am.''

"Good.'' Alison had to force herself to breathe. "Maybe before long you'll be settled.''

"And you can start decorating that nursery you've been so anxiously waiting for.''

"Yes.'' She didn't look at him; she was digging in the back of her closet for her black velvet cape. "I'd better be going, Logan. Have a good time with your parents.''

"I will.''

He followed her downstairs, but at a distance; Alison was already in the living room, where the elder Kavanaughs were watching television, when Logan reached the foot of the stairs. She took one look at the screen and rolled her eyes. There, in living color, were the final seconds of the

Zoo Baby story—the footage of mother and child safe in a hospital bed.

"He didn't force you to watch that, did he?" The question, directed as much at Logan as his parents, promised reprisals if he'd been the instigator.

Camilla Kavanaugh was laughing. "How perfectly delightful! Heavens, no, I'd heard about it from a friend who lives here, and I asked if there was a copy around. So you're just as nutty about zoos as Logan is? I knew this was a perfect match!"

Alison didn't even bother to answer that. She said her goodbyes instead, told Camilla that she'd love Cicero's, and was putting her hand on the doorknob when Logan said, "Just a second, Alison."

With his long, lazy stride, he was beside her almost before she saw him coming. Her cape kept her from fending him off; one of his hands came to rest squarely between her shoulder blades and pulled her toward him. "If I'm careful not to smudge your lipstick...?" He didn't wait for an answer to the half question.

The kiss started off gently, as if it really was the commonplace goodbye it pretended to be. But it didn't stay that way. The first taste of her seemed to inflame Logan; he muttered something, in a voice so low it was little more than a growl, and pulled her closer. His kiss held both demand and promise, sweetness and a piquancy that made her tingle—and by the time he raised his head Alison thought a sudden dense fog had settled in the living room. Everything looked hazy and slightly gray, and she was having trouble breathing, as if the air had grown immensely heavy.

Logan's mother, she saw, was beaming.

No wonder. That, she admitted, had been a very effective bit of stagecraft. Good thing she'd recognized it in time, for it had almost convinced Alison herself.

* * *

The ballroom of the Englin Hotel was one of the oldest and most luxurious public spaces in Chicago. Constructed in the grand, expansive era just after the enormous fire which had gutted the city and released the entrepreneurs to build from the ground once more, it had been left in its original state over the years. In a modern age which couldn't reproduce such grandeur at any cost, the ballroom still featured acres of gilt trim, enormous crystal chandeliers, elaborate paintings on the arched ceiling.

Waiters were hurrying to set up the round banquet tables on the ballroom floor; the head table was already in place along one side, and three enormous television screens had been placed so every person in the room would have an excellent view of the video.

Alison checked out every arrangement. The machinery worked perfectly; the screens and speakers were at precisely the correct angles; the sound level was high enough to let every word and note of music be heard, without blasting anyone's eardrums. And in a locked room nearby, three thousand copies of the videotape waited to be handed out as the guests left.

Everything was as perfect as it could be. Now all she had to do was wait—through the interminable social hour, through the same basic dinner menu as every other banquet she'd ever attended, through the after-dinner speeches of the city leaders who had conceived and financed this project. Only then would it be her turn.

The guests were gathering; she asked the bartender for a club soda and sipped it as she circulated among the crowd.

Midway through the cocktail hour, Kit swooped up to give her a hug. "Nice earrings, Ali. You're going to knock 'em dead, you know."

"Keep telling me," Alison said gloomily. "Now that it's too late, I can think of a hundred ways to improve that thing."

"Of course you can. You work on every project straight up till the last minute, till they come and take it away and you can't work anymore. And the results are always great, Ali." Her gaze skimmed the crowd. "Sue's supposed to be here, somewhere. My beloved stood me up—can you believe it? Just because he had to go to Atlanta for some kind of business emergency—so Sue told Marc she was going to be my date so he didn't have to come, either."

"I'll bet he threw a real fuss at being left behind," Alison said dryly.

Kit laughed. "He was broken-hearted at having to watch the sports channel instead, believe me."

One of the video's backers came up to talk to Alison, and Kit waved a casual hand and plunged into the crowd. "Are you *certain* you don't want to be at the head table?" the backer asked Alison anxiously. "You've been a lot more important to the outcome of this project than most of the fuddie-duddies who are up there to be stared at."

Alison laughed. "That's exactly why I don't want to be up there. I don't like being stared at."

"Well, now that you mention it... Isn't your husband with you? I'm dying to meet him—what a romantic hero he must be."

The ratings on the Zoo Baby story must be thrilling the television station, Alison thought. Everybody in greater Chicago had seen it a half dozen times. "He certainly is a hero," she said. "But I'm afraid he's not here tonight. Another obligation kept him from—"

"Being on time," Logan said smoothly, and slid an arm around Alison to keep her drink from tipping out of her hand.

He looked even better in a tuxedo than he did in scrubs, Alison thought faintly. Which in her opinion was saying a great deal.

"What are you... Did you just park your parents some-where? Logan, you can't simply—"

"They're over at the bar."

"You brought them? They'll hate it. And what about tickets? The guest list is so tight that—"

"I borrowed one from Kit and one from Susannah."

"So that explains why they're a twosome tonight. Is Kit's husband really out of town?"

"How should I know? That took care of Mom and Dad, and I talked myself in on the strength of being with you. I do hope you haven't given my ticket away?"

Alison shook her head, and his long, slow smile made her heart turn over. *It isn't fair,* Alison thought. *He doesn't even have to touch me...*

"Good," he said. "Otherwise I'd have made you sit on my lap and share your dinner."

The executive giggled. Alison, reminded that they had an audience, felt herself turning red.

The Kavanaughs came over, drinks in hand. Logan's father was also wearing a tux, and his mother was elegant in a long pink gown which set off her silvery hair to perfection. The clothes alone told Alison this hadn't been a last-minute decision.

"I hope you're not annoyed with us for showing up," Camilla said. "Logan told us how concerned you were that we'd be bored—but my dear, how can it possibly be boring to see your work?"

"It's hardly Hollywood, Camilla." Alison nibbled at her lower lip. "I hope you won't be disappointed."

"Disappointed?" Camilla said softly. "In you?"

Deep inside Alison the ice cube that she'd carried for so long began to melt, its edges slowly softening until it no longer cut at her with every breath she took.

This, she thought, *is what a family should be.*

The glow of approval in Camilla's eyes carried Alison

through dinner and the program. When the lights were turned down and the television screens came to life, she didn't even know she was nibbling at her thumbnail until Logan captured her hand and held it tightly between both of his.

The video rolled, and the city she so loved sprang to life on the screens. In the snow, under fallen leaves, with the promise of spring—Chicago was beautiful anytime.

But the city was more than the pretty pictures the video used to draw the audience in. Business, industry, resources, workers, the transportation network—all took their part in the story. And if at the end there was a single person who wasn't convinced that Chicago was the best and only place for a new business to be, it wasn't apparent in the ballroom of the Englin Hotel. Silence accompanied the darkness at the end of the video, but it lasted only a moment; as the lights came up, so did the crowd, three thousand people surging to their feet with a roar of appreciation.

Alison didn't hear it, and she saw only two things. One was Camilla Kavanaugh's warm smile, a smile which held approval and appreciation, but not the slightest hint of surprise.

The other was the warmth in Logan's eyes as he looked down at her, her hand still caught between his, and said, "Not bad, Novak. Not bad at all."

She thought it was quite possibly the best prize she'd ever won.

She dreamed of the birthday party again that night. This time the cake had four candles, and she managed to carry it all the way across the room and set it in front of the child—a child with long, glossy dark hair and big green eyes in which the candle flames reflected like stars.

Green eyes, Alison thought in bemusement. She'd never seen any color in the dreams before, but this time it wasn't like old, brittle home-movie footage. It was more like a modern video...

The child stared at the cake, and then a voice behind Alison said, "Smile for Daddy, honey," and the little girl grinned, and Alison turned slowly around...

And woke, knowing that if she had held on to the threads of her dream for one more instant, it would have been Logan she saw holding the camera.

Tears so hot they scorched her skin trickled down over her temples and lost themselves in her hair.

Sometimes you don't seem to need anyone, Kit had told her once. Insightful though Kit was, she'd been wrong that time. Alison did need another person in her life—someone to love, and to love her in return—and she'd known it for a long time.

She'd thought that person was a child. A child she could protect and cherish. A child whom no one else could claim or hurt. A child who would belong only to her.

Now she knew she'd been wrong. She still wanted a baby; there was no doubt in her mind about that. But she understood now that it wasn't just any child who could satisfy that need. And it wasn't a child alone.

Once, she had caught herself thinking of Logan as the ideal father of her baby, and she'd thought the idea hilarious. It wasn't funny anymore. It wasn't funny at all.

"Awake?" he said softly, and Alison froze, for the source of the voice in the darkness was only inches away.

She'd almost forgotten he was there beside her. In fact, when she'd gone to sleep, still hugging tight the pleasant memories of the evening, he hadn't been there; he'd been on the phone downstairs, checking on one of his patients. Perhaps he'd even gone to the hospital. At any rate, he must have come upstairs much later, long after she'd drifted into oblivion.

"Bad dream," she said. She sounded as if she were choking.

"It must have been. You were thrashing around and crying..." He raised himself on one elbow.

In the faint glimmer of a quarter moon she could see little more than a shape. It was imagination which showed her the tousled hair, the sleep-shadowed eyes, the ripple of muscles in his arms and bare chest...

His fingertips caught the last trace of tears, and his palm cupped her cheek. "And talking about the baby."

She closed her eyes, but that didn't shut out the sensations, only allowed the sweet scent of soap which clung to his skin to torment her instead. "Talking...what did I say?"

"Something about wondering how long it'll be."

She breathed a grateful sigh. It could have been a whole lot worse. "It does seem like forever sometimes."

"It doesn't have to be."

She started to sit up. Her breasts brushed his arm, and she drew back. But somehow she'd pulled him off balance, too. Suddenly he was lying close beside her, and though he wasn't touching her at all anymore—not even his hand against her face—the very air between them crackled with a million volts of power.

Alison managed a wry note in her voice. "If you're offering the good old-fashioned way..."

She could feel, more than see, his shrug. "Isn't that what you had in mind?" His husky murmur was like hands coated with warm oil sliding across her skin. But this touch didn't soothe, it inflamed. It excited. It almost hurt.

But it didn't surprise.

The fact that she didn't feel shocked by his question told her something else about herself. *You set this up when you invited his parents to stay,* she admitted. *You wanted it to happen.*

And now, what she had—unconsciously, perhaps, but no less earnestly—desired had come to be. All she had to do was reach out to him.

But something held her back. Some gremlin in the back of her mind whispered, *Why?*—and wariness crept out of the closet she'd so briefly managed to lock it into.

"All the objections I told you about before still apply." She hardly recognized her own voice. All her natural firmness was gone; though she was making a statement, it was so tentative as to be a question. Would he argue over those objections? The situation had changed so much for her; had it for him?

He raised up on one elbow again. "You mean you don't have a contract already written up and stashed under your pillow?"

Was that the barest hint of laughter in his voice? Not that it mattered; the question alone told her all she needed to know.

A lot of men would think that kind of deal was pretty inviting, he'd told her once. *They could have all the fun and none of the responsibility.*

He'd certainly thought it through fast enough then. Perhaps he would even have volunteered, if she hadn't made it painfully clear that she wasn't interested. But now...

Even his mother was less of a concern than before; with his job search going well, he could be gone long before Camilla ever suspected a pregnancy.

He'd have to be blind not to know that if he played his cards right he could have the fun, and duck the responsibility. And Alison was bitterly disappointed to think that he found that combination attractive.

"I told you," she said. "Contracts can be overthrown. Courts have minds of their own. It would be practically impossible for you to sign away your rights."

And she held her breath.

She wanted him to say, *Contracts be damned. Any rights I have, I keep.*

Any rights at all—whether those rights concerned their child, or Alison herself...

For a moment which seemed to stretch into years, he was as silent and still as an effigy. Then he shook his head a little and said, "All very true. Even the easy way has its complications, doesn't it? It's your choice, of course—and how wise of you not to let anything distract you from your goal."

He turned his back on her.

Alison lay absolutely still and tried to pretend she was alone. As indeed she was—for though they were side by side, they were also a million miles apart.

CHAPTER TEN

ALISON would have sworn she didn't sleep, but the ring of the telephone was no more than an unpleasant buzz nagging at her like a pesky housefly. The first thing she heard clearly was Logan's voice, low and husky.

"I'll be right there," he said, and added something long, involved, and Latin-sounding which she supposed had to do with medications.

It was not long past dawn, and she debated whether to take the easy route and pretend to be asleep until after he'd left the room. But she would have had to face him sometime, and if he caught her playing possum he might get the idea that she was regretting what had happened—or, to be more precise, *hadn't* happened—during the night. So she sat up and started to plump her pillows into shape as a backrest.

He was pulling a shirt from the closet; he glanced over his shoulder at her but didn't say a word.

Deliberately, she let her gaze rove over him. There was nothing she hadn't seen before, though she had to admit that the silky pajama pants which rode low on his narrow hips offered an even more intriguing view than the other things she'd seen him wearing. The rest was the same— broad shoulders with plenty of muscle, trim waist...

He tossed the shirt and a pair of trousers across the end of the bed and reached for the drawstring of his pajamas.

Only rigid self-control kept Alison from plunging under the blankets and burying her head. Instead she reached for a book from the nightstand, flipped it open on her lap, and frowned down at the page. She didn't lift her gaze even when Logan, fully dressed but buttoning his cuffs, came to stand over her. "Interesting reading," he said.

"I think so."

"Most people wouldn't dare study economic theory in bed. It's hard enough to stay awake for it in a classroom."

Was he teasing her? Alison stared up at him, but she couldn't detect so much as a hint of humor in his eyes, only cool disinterest. That made her feel sad; if even the laughter was gone...

She might as well face up to it. Nothing was going to be the same. The next few weeks would have been difficult enough, no matter what, but after last night...

"I'll be at the hospital." Logan settled his collar. "And I have no idea when I'll be back."

She wanted to ask about his patient. There was a note in his voice which made her think this was going to be a difficult—maybe dangerous—birth.

But he'd probably think she was just being nosy. Or that she was trying to keep him beside her for another minute... "I'll give your parents the message."

He shrugged. "They'll understand. It was pretty much a miracle that nobody had a crisis all day yesterday, so this was to be expected."

He made every effort to be quiet, but Alison's hearing had grown hypersensitive where he was concerned. She lay back against her pillows and listened to each light footfall on the stairs, to the creak of the closet door as he reached for a jacket, to the soft hush of the front door closing behind him.

And she told herself not to be an idiot. She'd made the right choice last night, the only choice she could make.

Still...

If she had turned to him last night, the next weeks would have been no less difficult. In some ways, they'd be even worse; she'd have had to pretend that making love with him was no more to her than a casual fling, one more way to pleasantly pass the time until they could go their separate ways. And that pretense wouldn't be simply a mask to be assumed now and then. She would have to live the part— even though every minute of the charade would have hurt her as badly as sandpaper against a sunburn.

But there would have been compensations for that pain. The moments of pleasure they shared would have been, for her, memories to hold close forever. And if their actions resulted in a child...

Well, that wasn't going to happen, was it? She'd made her choice, and having second thoughts didn't mean that her decision had been the wrong one. Besides, just now she had other things to do. She had to get dressed, go downstairs, entertain Logan's parents, see them off.

She certainly didn't have time to cry.

Alison had been right about one thing—the following two weeks were difficult. In fact, they were next door to impossible, because her own emotions were in such an upheaval that she could hardly tell up from down. At the end of each day she didn't know whether to be grateful that another twenty-four hours had passed, or sorry that the still-shadowy end was that much closer.

It wasn't really anything Logan did which made the days so difficult. True, he didn't bring her coffee in the mornings anymore, even when she dawdled in her room instead of coming downstairs. There were no more invitations to dinner or to the zoo—but then she wasn't issuing any, either.

He was unfailingly polite, and he did his full share around the house. In fact, if it hadn't been for an extra coffee cup each morning and the fact that she never fed the cats anymore because he always beat her to the job, Alison would hardly have known he was there. There were several nights when he didn't come home at all, and she lay in the darkness and listened to the silence and told herself that it was really not her concern whether he was at the hospital or somewhere else.

With Sara Williams, perhaps. The surgeon had called once when Logan was out and rather than just leaving a message she'd chatted for a while with Alison. It was all very straightforward and civilized, and Alison would probably have accepted it at face value if Sara hadn't said, with a laugh, that she was jealous of Alison, now that she was the one getting regular foot rubs…

Alison gritted her teeth and told herself it meant nothing. So what if Logan had rubbed the woman's feet? They probably *hurt* after Sara had stood for hours in an operating room. There wasn't necessarily anything romantic about it; hadn't Sara said, when she came into the emergency room to examine Alison that night, that she had a date?

Alison tried not to remember Logan's reply, but the little demon in the back of her brain had taken note and could repeat it word for word: *You shouldn't be hanging around with that guy anyway, Sara.*

Was it only in friendship that he'd spoken? Or did he have a personal stake in who Sara Williams dated?

Alison reminded herself that it was none of her business. *But you'd like it to be,* the demon whispered. And she had to admit it; even that long ago, lying on her back in an emergency room, in horrible pain and on her way to surgery, she had been so intensely aware of Logan Kavanaugh that every word he'd said might as well have been tattooed on her heart.

She did indeed, she confessed, have it bad.

When he was gone, she thought about him and seemed to see him in every shadow. When he was there, it was tougher still; she didn't even have to be looking at him to see the sensual way his hands moved—the skilled, healing hands which could also, she knew, give exquisite pleasure...and would be doing so, if only she had made a different choice.

Camilla Kavanaugh wasn't helping matters. She was completely innocent, of course; her occasional telephone calls were brief and cheerful, she was always supportive and interested in Alison's doings. And with every conversation Alison felt worse. There was nothing she could do to prevent the hurt Camilla was eventually going to suffer. Oh, she could be rude, she supposed; that would start Camilla wondering, and perhaps then the final blow wouldn't come as such a shock.

But the truth was Alison was too weak to do anything of the sort, even in the name of kindness. Logan wasn't all she was going to lose; he would take with him the only hint she'd ever had of a real family. The moment Camilla understood that Alison was not the love of her son's life, not the wonderful woman he'd presented her as, not the new daughter she'd longed for, all that warm support—that budding love—would be gone. Still, Alison couldn't bring herself to give it up a moment before she had to.

She knew she was clinging to a fantasy. Right now it was the only thing she had to cling to.

The damned memo had to be there somewhere.

Alison sank into her chair and looked despairingly at the mess she'd made of her files. In some places, the top of her desk was six inches deep in paper. She'd turned every folder in her office inside out, and she still couldn't find the piece of letterhead she'd been looking for since lunch.

Susannah popped her head around the edge of the door. "Got a minute? What are you doing, anyway? Spring cleaning?"

"I seem to have misplaced a memo."

"Honeymoon-based amnesia," Susannah said wisely.

"Happens to all of us. You'll get over the worst of the absentmindedness in a month or two."

I should be so lucky, Alison thought.

Susannah sank into the wicker chair. "Ali, I have a confession to make. I know where that gift certificate came from."

"What gift certificate?" Alison started methodically searching a folder for the third time.

"The one for Logan's membership in the Chicago Singles."

"I always thought you had something to do with it."

"*Au contraire,* darling. Marc confessed. It seems the love of Kit's life got the idea and talked my beloved into chipping in."

"Why?"

Susannah waved a casual hand. "As Marc put it—and I quote—'Why should Logan escape... I mean, miss out on...all the joys of being married?'"

Alison gave a sharp, almost humorless laugh.

Susannah's eyebrows raised, but she went straight on. "I think it also had something to do with trying to hand-pick the third member of the trio. As close as you and Kitty and I are, they knew whoever you married was going to be around a lot, so naturally they assumed they should have something to say about it..." She turned her head as a tall form appeared in the doorway. "Well, well—if it isn't Logan. We were just speaking of you."

Alison had known he was coming. The instant she heard his familiar footsteps on the stairs, her heart started to pound painfully against her ribs. He hadn't come to Tryad in weeks, since shortly before the wedding. The fact that he was here, at midafternoon...

"Hello, Susannah," Logan said politely. "I'll wait in the kitchen if you—"

Susannah rose with a dancer's grace. "Heavens, no. I

wouldn't dream of keeping you two apart. Would you like me to hang a Do Not Disturb sign on the door as I leave?'' She smiled gently and drifted out.

Logan closed the door behind her and came toward Alison's desk. ''I've got good news.''

She tried to keep her voice steady. ''You've found a new job.'' She'd known as soon as she heard him on the stairs what must have happened. Nothing less would have brought him here, in the middle of the day. Nothing less would have made him seek her out.

''It's a good opportunity. Even if it wasn't for Burt Sinclair's little idiosyncracies, I'd have found this position enormously appealing. A younger group of doctors, a very progressive attitude...''

''That's wonderful.'' Alison shifted a stack of papers. ''I'm very pleased for you.''

''I told Burt I'd stay another three weeks—that lets me finish out a good many of my obligations and switch the remaining patients to other doctors.''

''But now it doesn't matter what he thinks anymore.'' She prided herself on how calm she sounded. It was a minor miracle, considering that every nerve in her body was jumping like drops of water on a hot griddle.

''Technically, I suppose not.''

''You sound a little doubtful.'' Or was that the right word? Was he...could he be...reluctant to bring this pretense to an end? If that was so, then anything could be possible. Alison's throat tightened.

''We've come so far that I'd hate to give him reason to talk just now.''

All her newborn hope trickled away. She felt empty.

''After the switch is official, it won't matter,'' Logan went on. ''Anything he says will just look like sour grapes. But till then—''

' "Of course." She knew her voice sounded dull, lifeless. She didn't care anymore.

"But just as soon as I've actually made the move—"

It hurt too much to think about it. She didn't even want to consider which would hurt worse—the upcoming three weeks, or the inevitable end. But in fact it was neither, she realized. It was his enthusiasm that stung her like a million angry bees. Dammit, did he have to be *eager* to get away?

She interrupted. "I understand. Three more weeks and we can stop pretending."

Logan looked at her for a long moment. "I was talking about the baby," he said. "The minute I'm in the new practice, where the records don't matter—"

She had forgotten about the baby. The child she had wanted so badly. The reason she'd gotten into this mess in the first place.

She looked down at the folder she held. The edges were bent where she had gripped it, damp from her nervous palms. "Oh," she said. "That."

"Yes, dammit, *that.*"

Alison laid the folder carefully aside. "I won't hold you to your promise." The silence was so dense it hurt her eardrums, and finally she couldn't stand it anymore. "The business is picking up, with the video's success... Now's probably not a good time. Maybe..." She swallowed hard. "Maybe someday I'll just adopt."

"I see," he said quietly. "I won't keep you away from your work any longer."

She waited till she heard Tryad's front door close behind him. Then she sank slowly deeper into her chair, as if she were melting. She put her head in her hands, heedless of the papers which her tears fell on and splattered and stained.

She didn't know anyone was in the room until Susannah's arms went around her. "Oh, my dear—"

"Go ahead and say it," Alison said drearily. "You reserved the right, remember, to say *I told you so* when it all fell apart."

Susannah said nothing at all. She knelt there on the floor and held Alison until at last the tears stopped.

A little later, Kit came in. "Ali, Rita sent me down to warn you—" She stopped dead in the doorway for a moment, eyes wide. "Well, I know it's not the television talk show people that pushed you over the brink," she said finally, "because they're still upstairs trying to pump Rita and waiting to talk to you about letting them tape your first visit to the Zoo Baby."

Alison sniffed. "Too late. I went last week."

"I'm sure they wouldn't hesitate to fake it."

"The last thing Ali needs is a camera shoved in her face," Susannah said grimly.

"She looks as if she's ill. Ali, what's—"

"Oh, yeah? Well, don't call your pal Logan for advice this time, because she was just fine till he showed up." Susannah gave Alison's shoulders a last squeeze. "I think a little diversion is called for. Kitty will draw off the sharks—"

"Oh, joy," Kit said.

"—And I'll run interference in case one of them eludes her. You, Ms. Novak, will make a dash for home, draw the blinds, and put yourself to bed. We'll hang on to the predators as long as we can, to give you a start, and then we'll ditch them and come over to check on how you're doing."

Alison shook her head. "You two are the limit. How I ever got lucky enough to find you—"

"An excellent question," Susannah said. Her eyes were sparkling with laughter. "But we can take up the discussion of who's luckiest some other time."

Alison managed a smile. "I'll be fine, once I'm home.

Please—you don't have to come and guard me. I'm not going to do something crazy.''

"That's good. Though I'll reserve judgment about what you might consider crazy," Kit murmured. "Do you have a plan for how I distract the hyenas, Sue, or shall I wing it?"

"I have enormous faith in your creativity," Susannah said solemnly. "But you might try to entice them into the conference room, so Ali can slide out the front door."

"I'd rather go into an arena with a bull," Kit muttered. She swept a deep bow and stalked off toward the stairs.

Alison started packing folders into her briefcase. She'd need something to keep her hands busy; she might as well spend the rest of the day searching for the elusive memo, and perhaps the hours wouldn't be completely wasted after all.

A couple of minutes later the intercom buzzed. "The coast's clear for the moment," Rita hissed.

Susannah said, "Are you absolutely certain you'll be all right?"

No, Alison thought. *But I'm dead sure I don't want company.* "I'm fine. A little rest, a couple of aspirin—"

"—And call me in the morning," Susannah said dryly. "Okay, let's run for it."

She went upstairs first, and by the time Alison tiptoed past Rita's office, Susannah had pulled the huge copy machine out from the wall, parked it squarely in the arched doorway, and started poking around at the back of it. A three-year-old couldn't have slid past, much less a camera crew.

Alison sent her a thumbs-up sign and strolled out into the sunshine.

There were only a couple of mothers with small children in the park; Alison waved and went on by. Perhaps, despite the sun, it was a little too chilly for babies to be out. Or maybe it was simply nap time.

She wasted a couple of blocks in speculation before, with regret, she turned her thoughts back to her own difficulties.

Three more weeks. But would they be three more endless weeks to get through, or three more precious weeks to savor?

Just what kind of a question was that? She'd endure, because that was all she could do.

And yet...he'd said it was her choice.

Yes, she argued, but she'd already made that choice. He'd edged away from responsibility, and that in itself...

That, she reminded herself, was exactly what she'd wanted in the first place. Why wasn't she content with it now?

Perhaps it was because she'd been asking the wrong question. No matter how much she wanted him, it wasn't in her power to make Logan care about her; she might as well waste her time wishing for the moon. But if she asked herself instead whether or not she wanted his child...

There was only one possible answer to that.

She let herself into the row house, and knew immediately—despite the silence—that he was there. It took her a moment to spot him because he was so still; he was stretched out in an overstuffed chair, feet sprawling, head back, both cats curled up in his lap. He didn't look at ease, but more like a rag doll tossed down by a careless child.

She crossed the living room and stood in front of him. She knew she would have to do this quickly, and right away; if she stopped to think she'd never finish the question. "Logan," she said softly. "I was a little rattled when you were in my office."

His gaze moved slowly down over her body, but for once she didn't feel sensuality in his scrutiny, only cold inspection.

"I said a couple of really foolish things," she went on. "Of course I still want a baby. It's what I want most of all—the center of my life. But—" She bit her lip and looked straight at him and lied. "What you said about office records, about how anybody could look on my chart and know…"

His tone was dry. "We don't exactly post patients' charts in the Internet, Alison."

"Well, it made me think, anyway. And I've decided…" She had to stop and swallow hard. "That maybe the old-fashioned way is best after all."

"And you want my approval? I can't imagine why you think you need it, but—"

"I want your cooperation."

He threw his head back against the chair. "Oh, that's rich. *Now* you've decided you want my baby? What brought you to this insight, Alison? Did it suddenly occur to you that I'm such a workaholic I wouldn't have time to interfere even if I wanted to—so you'd be safe?"

Well, she hadn't exactly expected that he'd be thrilled, had she? And she'd already known his feelings on responsibility—so it was foolish to feel just a bit disappointed.

"Have you got the contract all written out?" He didn't wait for an answer. He leaped up.

Despite her intentions of standing firm, Alison backed a step away.

But he didn't seem to notice. He didn't come closer to her; he started instead to pace the living room. "So I'm the winner of the lottery after all. How delightful. What an honor. Is that why you wanted to get closer to my parents— so you could check out the gene pool?"

"You don't have to be crude," she snapped. "Just—yes or no. Which is it?"

For an instant the world seemed to hang in the balance.

"No," he said. "Absolutely not. Forget it."

Alison's heart slammed to her toes. She told herself to walk away with dignity. But the words were out before she could stop herself. "You would have, once. You wanted—"

"That was when I thought you were human—or at least had the potential to be. Now that I know for certain you're nothing more than a computer chip with a screwball virus—"

She shrank under the fierce lash of his words. "I just thought…" But there was no point in going on. Her shoulders slumped and she looked down at her hands, fingers twisted. With the last threads of her dignity, she pulled the two rings—the diamond cluster and her wedding ring—off and held them out to him.

"I'd appreciate it if you…went away," she said. "As far as anybody needs to know, everything's just as it has been. But I can't… I just can't…" Her voice broke. She tossed the rings down on the coffee table and turned toward the stairs and the safety of her room.

"Alison, wait." The lash was gone from his voice. "Why?"

She knew he wasn't asking about why she'd told him to leave, but about the child. She didn't look back at him. "I told you. Being a mother is important to me."

"That's not really an answer. Why my child?"

She couldn't tell him the truth, and she hadn't thought of an excuse. Silently, she shook her head.

She didn't know how near he'd moved until his words stirred the hairs at the nape of her neck. "Because of this?" His lips brushed the soft triangle below her ear, and Alison gasped.

Gently, but inexorably, he turned her to face him. She took one look at him and closed her eyes in order to shut out the fire that flashed in his.

But she couldn't turn off the rest of her senses. Touch,

as his hands skimmed over her shoulders, down her back, drawing her close. Scent, as she tried to draw in the breath she needed and the soft aroma of soap and aftershave hit her in a rush instead. Taste, as his mouth came down on hers, tantalizingly gentle, and then fierce as he read her surrender.

He's taking his revenge, she thought. But she didn't care. If this was to be the last kiss, she would drown herself in it, so she would never forget...

She didn't know how long he kissed her, only that her brain was reeling and she couldn't remember what it was like to breathe by the time he eased a half inch away from her and whispered, "Is it only a child you want?"

She choked on the words. "I thought...that's all I can have. You want the fun without the responsibility—all right. I'll live with that—"

He shook her just a little, till she stopped talking. "Where did you get that idea?"

"You said..." She gulped. "You said that a lot of men would. You joked that night—about me having a contract ready. And you *offered*—"

"Only because I believed you'd given up all that nonsense, that you'd realized the harsh and empty life you'd described wasn't what you wanted after all." He held her away from him and looked down at her, his eyes narrowed. "When I have a child, Alison, you can bet your soul on me being there. And I'm not talking about the delivery room, I'm talking about everything. Nobody will ever succeed in cutting me out of that child's life. And until the time I'm certain that nobody is ever going to try, there will be no child of mine in this world."

She gulped. It was everything she'd wanted him to say, and yet...

There was still an ice cube lodged deep within her. The edges had gone the night of the video premiere, melted in the pride and approval he and his parents had shown her. But a cold chunk still remained, buried beneath her heart, an uncomfortable reminder that he hadn't actually said he wanted *her*, just that he would never give up his child.

"I watched you," he said, "with that little girl at the zoo, with my parents. Those things told me that hard, bitter woman who was so afraid of being hurt that she wouldn't take a chance on loving wasn't really you. Yes, there was that business with your mother—but when I thought about it, I realized it was more of an explanation than a difficulty."

She frowned. "You said you thought it was none of your business."

"And it isn't," he agreed. "At least not the exact reason you don't want to talk to her. I just knew there had to be one—a good one—and that it helped explain why you were so afraid of loving anyone. Why you wanted so much space around you—not only in your bed and in those oversize nightshirts that are so incredibly sexy, but in your life."

She felt a tinge of color rise. He'd only really looked at her nightshirt once. She had thought he'd stopped looking because he didn't find them—or her—appealing.

"It wasn't long after my announcement to Burt Sinclair before I had to admit I was enjoying it all far too much—teasing you, kissing you, holding you. Bringing you coffee in the morning and watching you, all soft and tender and sleepy, before you took on the world again. But every time I let myself start to dream, you jolted me back to reality. You were so eager for me to find a new job so you could be rid of me, and so pleased today when I told you the news..."

She shook her head.

"And then," he said softly, "you wouldn't even accept my help to have the child you want so badly. Much less accept *me*."

She reached up to touch the white line on his lip—as if by soothing that scar she could also ease the wounds that didn't show. "Now I know it was never just a baby that I wanted. It was love. But I thought there was no one—"

"Who could love you? Oh, my darling..." He kissed her gently. "What did your mother do to make you believe that?"

Alison sighed and closed her eyes and told him what she had never shared with anyone before. "She left, when I was five. Now I know there was another man. Then, I couldn't understand what I'd done to make her leave me. It must have been awfully bad—whatever I'd done—because no one would talk about it."

Logan's lips brushed her temple.

"My father... I resemble her, you see. So every time he looked at me I must have been a reminder. Salt rubbed into the wound. And later when he married again, to a woman who already had her own children..."

His arms tightened around her, as if he could protect her from the pain. "And favored them?"

Alison nodded. "She—my mother—came back to visit me when I was nine, I think. She threatened my father, that she'd take me. I was thrilled—till I found out she didn't mean it. He bought her off, not because he wanted me but so she couldn't hold him up for money to raise me."

He nestled her even closer against his chest.

"I was so unhappy I begged her to let me go with her after all. But she only laughed and said I'd be in the way, and now that she had what she wanted..." She paused, till the ache in her throat eased enough so she could draw a full breath again. "I didn't see her again till I was sixteen...and then once more a couple of years ago when my father died."

He said something, half under his breath, about what

should be done to incompetent parents, and Alison felt a little more of the ice cube deep inside her trickle away.

''I suppose that's why I want a child,'' she admitted. ''To prove I can be a better mother than mine was.''

''*That*,'' Logan said grimly, ''isn't even a fit question for you to be asking.'' He held her away from him. ''Now, let's get things straight. You're not the one who's setting the terms of this contract anymore, because I have a few requirements of my own. For one thing, it's going to include marriage—not the sort we've had up to now, but a marriage that lasts till death do us part. I love you, Alison. I want to spend my life with you.''

''I love you, too.'' But her voice quavered uncertainly.

''What is it?'' he asked gently.

She shook her head a little. ''My parents loved each other once. And look what they did—''

''Your parents were incapable of loving—each other, or you. To do what they did to an innocent child...to use you in their war...no wonder you were determined not to let any man have that kind of hold over you.'' His voice was husky. ''Alison—can you trust that I will never do that to you?''

She looked up into his face, and saw love and tenderness, compassion and concern. And she felt a sort of itch deep inside, as if the long-hidden wounds were starting to heal.

''Or to our child,'' she whispered, and stood on her toes to kiss the tiny scar on his lip as if to seal the promise.

After a while, he said softly, ''Do you want your flute player back? You can wear him for luck.''

''Then you did know.''

''About it being a fertility charm? Of course. It was still a joke, then.''

''When did it stop being one?''

''At the zoo,'' he said thoughtfully. ''At least, that was where I knew it—it had been happening all along, but I didn't want to admit it. But then there was the message from your mother—and I had to face the fact that to you, how I felt wasn't important at all."

"It was *too* important. But I didn't realize it for a while. Till that silly party, when you came in—"

The telephone began to ring, and Logan protested when she pulled away. "It'll be either Sue or Kitty," she warned, "and if I don't answer, they'll be over here in five minutes flat to check on me."

"Five minutes?" Logan grinned and gave her a little push. "Then by all means, answer."

It was Susannah. "Are you doing all right?"

"I'm fine, Sue. I'm—"

Logan blew gently on the nape of Alison's neck, sending a delightful shiver down her spine, and then started nibbling at her throat.

"I'm great," Alison managed.

"You sound like you're shaking with cold—but that's not surprising, with the shock you've suffered. Do you have a hot water bottle?"

Alison stifled a giggle. "I think I can find something that will keep me warm. Thanks, Sue—but can I talk to you later?" She put the telephone down, and once more Logan drew her close.

He ran a gentle hand over her hair, tangled his fingers into the glossy black mass, and turned her face up to his. "You asked me once to help you have a baby," he mused.

Alison let the very last shard of ice buried deep within her melt—and before he was finished kissing her, it had turned to steam.

"Honey," he said unsteadily, "I'd be delighted."

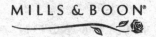

MILLS & BOON®

Makes
any time
special

Enjoy a romantic novel from
Mills & Boon®

Presents™ *Enchanted*™ *Temptation*

Historical Romance™ *Medical Romance*™

MILLS & BOON®

Next Month's Romance Titles

♡

Each month you can choose from a wide variety of romance novels from Mills & Boon®. Below are the new titles to look out for next month from the Presents™ and Enchanted™ series.

Presents™

Enchanted™

On sale from 8th January 1999

H1 9812

Available at most branches of WH Smith, Tesco, Asda, Martins, Borders and all good paperback bookshops

MILLS & BOON®

Medical Romance™

COMING NEXT MONTH

SARAH'S GIFT by Caroline Anderson
Audley Memorial Hospital

Having lost her own family, Sarah loved having Matt Ryan
and his little girl, Emily, living with her while they were in
England. She didn't know that Matt had an inestimable
gift for her...

POTENTIAL DADDY by Lucy Clark

Kathryn wasn't sure she liked the professional Jack—brilliant
and arrogant—but his private side was a revelation. He'd
make the perfect father, but who would he choose as the
mother of his potential children?

LET TOMORROW COME by Rebecca Lang

Gerard came to Jan's help when she most needed it, but she
found it so hard to trust, she was sure he'd have a hidden
agenda. How could he convince her that he hadn't?

THE PATIENT MAN by Margaret O'Neill

Harry Paradine knew if he was patient enough that the right
woman would come along. When she finally did, he found
Emily Prince less than trustful—but why?

*Available at most branches of WH Smith, Tesco, Asda,
Martins, Borders, Easons, Volume One/James Thin
and most good paperback bookshops*

LYNN ERICKSON

The Eleventh Hour

Jack Devlin is on Death Row, convicted of murdering his
beautiful socialite wife. But the evidence is too cut and dry
for lawyer Eve Marchand. When Jack escapes and
contacts Eve, she is forced to make a decision that
changes her life.

*"Lynn Erickson joins the ranks of Sandra Brown
and Nora Roberts"*

—The Paperback Forum

1-55166-426-7
**AVAILABLE IN PAPERBACK
FROM DECEMBER, 1998**

SHARON SALA

Tory Lancaster is a woman trying to
leave behind a legacy of abandonment and sorrow.
She is about to come face to face with her past. A past
she must confront if she is to have any
hope of possessing a future.

SWEET BABY

1-55166-416-X
AVAILABLE IN PAPERBACK
FROM DECEMBER, 1998

LINDA HOWARD

DIAMOND BAY

Someone wanted this man dead. He was barely alive as
he floated up to the shore. Shot twice and unconscious.
Rachel's sixth sense told her she was his only hope.
The moment she decided not to call the police
she decided his future. As well as her own.

"Howard's writing is compelling."

—Publishers Weekly

1-55166-307-4
AVAILABLE IN PAPERBACK
FROM DECEMBER, 1998

HOLLYWOOD
Heroes

We are giving away a year's supply of Mills & Boon® books to the five lucky winners of our latest competition. Simply match the six film stars to the films in which they appeared, complete the coupon overleaf and send this entire page to us by 30th June 1999. The first five correct entries will each win a year's subscription to the Mills & Boon series of their choice. What could be easier?

1

2

3

4

5

6

CABARET	__	**GONE WITH THE WIND**	__
ROCKY	__	**SMOKEY & THE BANDIT**	__
PRETTY WOMAN	__	**GHOST**	__

C8L

Please turn over for details of how to enter ➜

UR 2006

G4820

HOW TO ENTER

There are six famous faces and a list of six films overleaf. Each of the famous faces starred in one of the films listed and all you have to do is match them up!

As you match each one, write the number of the actor or actress who starred in each film in the space provided. When you have matched them all, fill in the coupon below, pop this page in an envelope and post it today. Don't forget you could win a year's supply of Mills & Boon® books—you don't even need to pay for a stamp!

Mills & Boon Hollywood Heroes Competition
FREEPOST CN81, Croydon, Surrey, CR9 3WZ
EIRE readers: (please affix stamp) PO Box 4546, Dublin 24.

Please tick the series you would like to receive if you are one of the lucky winners

Presents™ ❑ Enchanted™ ❑ Historical Romance™ ❑
Medical Romance™ ❑ Temptation® ❑

Are you a Reader Service™ subscriber? Yes ❑ No ❑

Ms/Mrs/Miss/Mr ....Initials ....
(BLOCK CAPITALS PLEASE)

Surname..

Address ....

....

.................................Postcode........................

(I am over 18 years of age) C8L

Closing date for entries is 30th June 1999. One entry per household. Free subscriptions are for four books per month. Competition open to residents of the UK and Ireland only. As a result of this application, you may receive further offers from Harlequin Mills & Boon and other carefully selected companies. If you would prefer not to share in this opportunity please write to The Data Manager at the address shown above.

Mills & Boon is a registered trademark of Harlequin Mills & Boon Ltd.